The Winged Fae

The World of Fae

Book 3

TERRY SPEAR

The Winged Fae

Copyright © 2011 Terry Spear

Published by Terry Spear

Cover Art by Terry Spear

ISBN-10: 1633110303
ISBN-13: 978-1633110304

DEDICATION

To those of us who have the ability to not take
ourselves so seriously and enjoy being frivolous every
once in a while, which plays into the world of the fae!

ACKNOWLEDGMENTS

Thanks to my readers who love the world of fae!

ABOUT THE WINGED FAE:

Niall, a royal member of the Denkar, aka the dark fae, is visiting South Padre Island when he catches a winged fae painting graffiti on a wall on the island claimed by his people. He is at once fascinated with the lovely girl and intrigued by her audacity, but as one of the Denkar, he must take her to task. Yet she's armed with a sleeping potion that makes his life intolerable. Between freeing her from his people's dungeon, her own tower, and fighting a knight in her honor, he wonders if he's lost his mind over one beautiful winged fae–when she's betrothed to his cousin!

CHAPTER 1

Niall released the door to the Tropics Ice Cream Shop in South Padre Island and headed outside into the humid warm breeze with only one thought: checking out the bathing beauties on the beach.

Until he spied a female winged fae boldly painting graffiti on a concrete block wall across the street. He stopped dead in his tracks.

Feeling a mixture of amusement and annoyance, he hated to admit he was highly intrigued as well. Frowning, he folded his arms and watched the winged fae paint broad, deliberate strokes on the Denkar fae's wall. Actually, the building belonged to humans, but when the fae were at South Padre Island, it—*and everything else on the island*—belonged to the Denkar.

Fae tended to be extremely territorial. Eons ago, they'd claimed this island way before humans had found it popular—except for maybe a passing pirate or two.

The only reason the dark fae had even allowed humans to live here was because they provided an infinite amount of entertainment for the fae. Sun bathing beauties. Sugar white beaches. Clear aquamarine waters. But the best part? The human women.

Of course, a female human often visited the island hand–in–hand with some guy. The fae took an inordinate amount of pleasure in separating the woman from the man, as was their roguish nature. Sometimes a female fae did the same as she latched onto a human male, creating conflict between the man and his girlfriend. Such was the immortal life of the fae. They had to do something to entertain themselves.

Niall considered the blond winged fae's clothes: a little black dress, gray–speckled tights and pink ballet slippers completing the impish outfit. She reminded him way more of a pixie or the legendary winged elf than a fae. Her blond hair was pulled back and a droopy pink satin ribbon was tied around her head. Droopy because of the heat and humidity late that afternoon on the beachfront property.

So what was a royal winged fae from the house of Mabara doing on South Padre Island, painting graffiti on a Denkar fae's block wall in broad daylight with her wings exposed?

She was gutsy. He'd give her that. Since his cousin Prince Deveron had slipped away with Alicia to avoid his mother's royal guard fetching him home, Niall had the day off. No reason to watch Deveron's back as his companion when Deveron was busy kissing Alicia somewhere else and no doubt wanted privacy.

Niall studied the fae's wings. As clear as they were, she was close to nineteen years of age. In a few more years, she could make them appear invisible to anyone who chanced to see her, either when she was showing herself off to humans or when she was in the fae realm. But to visit the human world during the late afternoon, wings prominently displayed for any human to see...what was she thinking?

Worse, she was visiting a site her kind *hadn't* claimed as their territory. And a royal Mabara fae at that. Rarely, if ever, did they leave the fae world before they could hide their wings.

Determining which fae house one of their kind came from was problematic at times, but not when they were winged and showed them off. Only four of the forty-two royal houses boasted royal winged fae, this one declaring the large raptor, the osprey, the symbol of their realm. Only the Mabara had wings with black lines crisscrossing it like a windowpane with delicate black edging.

Although she appeared cute and pixie–like, being a member of the Mabara's house meant she could be extremely dangerous if riled. Not that any fae couldn't be, and certainly his own kind—the lion fae—had a reputation as hunters, but the royal house of Mabara controlled the element of air.

The joke was that they could control air elementals,

but couldn't use the air to support their wings. Which had a lot to do with their kind having been so enamored with humans, they quit using their wings so they could move about like humans did. After centuries of disuse, their wings were no longer big enough or powerful enough to support them.

Pondering that she could call the wind to protect her or use it as an offensive weapon, Niall rubbed his chin. She didn't appear to have any real weapons on her, not that he could tell from the skimpy clothing she was wearing. The Mabara specialty was casting windstorms over the sea, creating waves of devastating proportions, or initiating powerful swirling wind funnels on land, even straight–line winds that could take out windows and windshields and walls made of brick.

More subtly, they could create a poisonous dust and blow it into the face of their foe that would kill their enemy. Mabara sometimes employed the use of a less lethal cocktail resulting in a couple of days of paralysis or a sleeping potion, both which contributed to the worst hangover a fae could suffer.

Not that Niall had ever gotten himself into such a bind. But he'd read about a case where a cobra fae had tangled with a Mabara royal fae, who had subsequently grown smitten with him. The man had dumped her for a fellow female cobra fae, and the Mabara wench had blasted him with the sleeping powder. For weeks, he'd had a devil of a time waking for any length of time. The royal houses had been at odds with one another ever since. It didn't take much for the fae kind to become sworn enemies.

Niall tried to figure out what strange symbols the girl was writing on the wall. But he couldn't determine what she was trying to say. It had to be a message for his kind though. And not a good one.

If he didn't put a stop to it, he would not be doing his duty to his people. He strode forth to take charge of the situation, and *her*.

But as soon as he began to move in her direction, he was certain she must have smelled his scent, because she whipped around, her soft pink lips parting and her blond brows raised in surprise—which almost made him smile to see her reaction—particularly knowing he had the upper hand.

"What do you think you're doing?" Niall asked sharply.

As soon as she turned to fully face him, she whipped a piccolo–looking wooden pipe out of a pocket that had been hidden from his sight. Poisoned fae dust.

He knew if he didn't make a hasty retreat and vanish in the blink of an eye, he could be one dead, dark fae.

***

Before Serena could stop what she was about to do, she'd blown the shimmering pink powder at the Denkar fae. Thank the goddess she had used the sleeping powder and not the one meant to take down an enemy— *permanently.* Although she had a reputation among the Mabara for creating the strongest sleeping concoction there was.

She didn't go on deadly missions because she wasn't even supposed to be visiting the human world, yet. Although she'd trained vigorously for the job. She always came prepared though. But she just couldn't stay away from them. Humans were just too intriguing—their interesting fashions, their modern conveniences, their non–conformity—when her own kind were stuck in the past with unbending tradition.

She was ever thankful her mother had never learned of her forays into the human world or the queen would have assigned guards to watch Serena's every move and ensured she didn't go where she wasn't supposed to. Like here.

She took a deep shuddering breath and considered the sleeping lion fae.

Oh, what had she done?

He'd startled her; that was the problem. It was all his fault he was lying on the ground, looking rather cherub like, his blond hair curling about his ears, his bright blue eyes closed now, his masculine lips parted slightly as he slept the sleep of the dead.

Her heart hammering, she quickly looked about, didn't see any sign of any other Denkar fae, but now her own efforts to attract one to send a further message to their kind was for naught.

She saw two bare–chested guys wearing knee–length, black and white floral swimming trunks and brown leather sandals, watching her from across the street in front of a beach shop. *Great.* She'd gathered an audience of humans instead of the dark fae.

"Cute wings," one guy said, giving her a thumb's up, his rusty–colored hair wet and curly. He motioned to the fae sleeping on the pavement. "What did you do to him?"

The human wasn't drawing any closer. Maybe because she had been painting graffiti on a building, and he didn't want to get too close in case the cops saw her. Or maybe he was afraid of her because she'd put a guy to sleep who had tried to stop her from painting on the wall.

She ignored the human, trying to figure out what to do with the Denkar fae. Oh well, she'd goofed, but there wasn't anything to do about it now. She turned around and finished painting her message to the dark fae.

Then she drew in close to the sleeping one and crouched next to him. She studied his long curly blond hair and his face. He had the same aristocratic look of the prince of the Denkar, same aquiline nose, same sturdy jaw as Crown Prince Deveron, except that this one was fair–haired while the other was dark. She wondered if they were related. She reached inside the fae's blue and green floral shirt—noting he was wearing dark blue swim trunks, too, the style long like the humans', his feet sporting a pair of navy flip–flops. Apparently, he had been enjoying South Padre Island like any human would before he came across her.

That was what she regretted most about her wings—

the inability to hide them and wear a bathing suit, while looking just like any other tourist on the beach. She longed to wear a hot pink bikini. Hot pink wasn't part of her usual fare and so, it just appealed. And a bikini? Scathing. Her mother would have fits if she even knew what Serena secretly wished to wear in front of a population of humans—or worse, in front of the fae—in particular, the dark fae.

Serena's fingers gingerly swept over the man's bare chest beneath his floral shirt, and she felt a thick chain. Sucking in her breath, she feared what it was sure to reveal. She pulled out a medallion. A symbol of the lion etched on the gold indicated he was ranked below the crown prince. He had to be a close companion of the prince, which meant this one was royalty also. A duke or earl or baron, no doubt.

She studied his masculine lips. And thought just how much havoc she could wreak if she kissed him. Served him right for startling her so.

Without analyzing whether she *should* do it, and just because she *could*, she pressed her mouth against his and gently kissed his lips, meaning only to give a quick peck and that was it. But his lips were soft and warm and inviting, not at all like she'd thought they would be. Despite not wishing it, she felt a tingly heat growing deep in her belly. She'd never kissed a man before, oh a boy, indeed several, yes, but this was different. She felt...something awakening that she couldn't quite fathom.

His lips curved up under hers and for a second, she thought he was awake, smiling at her kissing him. Her eyes widened as she pulled her mouth away from his. He hadn't kissed back. He was still asleep; not that she expected him to be awake. Truly, if he had been, she would have shrieked with panic. No one woke from that drug for at least a couple of days unless the Denkar had discovered an antidote. And then it could be as much as two months for the victim to fully shake off the effects, sometimes even longer, depending on how much resistance the body could garner.

Her thoughts reverted to the kiss and immediately the human faery tale *Sleeping Beauty* and the prince giving the princess a kiss to wake her sprang to mind. Why ever did humans make up such nonsense anyway?

She sat back on her haunches, frowning at him as he gave her the barest of smiles, his eyes still shut tight. She hadn't meant to give him anything pleasant to dream about. Annoyed with him for causing her to shoot him with the sleeping powder in the first place, she hit him in the shoulder with the flat of her hand. He frowned. He shouldn't have startled her.

She glanced back at the human males. They were both watching her with intrigue, but neither ventured any closer. "Cowards," she said under her breath.

If she took the Denkar with her, she could hide him for a couple of days, at least until he woke.

Or not. Where would she hide him but in her own kingdom? And if anyone found out, there would be the devil to pay. Both for her and for him.

She should leave him here. Let the Denkar find him. But they'd know that one of her kind had done this to him once they analyzed the shimmering pink dust on his hair and skin and clothes.

She glanced back at the wall. Well, the message couldn't be any clearer.

"Niall!" a woman called out, her voice sweet but worried at the same time. Commanding, too, as if she expected the fae to suddenly appear and bow down to her.

Serena whipped her head around and saw Ritasia, the Denkar princess, Deveron's sister, headed for a shop sporting beach wear, beach towels, and other touristy nick–nacks. The woman's dark hair was swept up into curls over her head, her eyes dark as midnight, while she wore typical royal attire—shimmering peach silk gowns flowing in the muggy breeze with every step she took, gold sandals, and a string of pearls woven into her hair. But no one could see her like the fae could as the princess moved about invisible to humans.

Uh–oh. Not good. Serena had meant for a lowly Denkar fae to discover her. Not all these lofty royals. She could twist a non–royal around her will, if he was not of the royal house. But the royal fae? Really not good.

As soon as the princess saw Serena with one dead–looking Denkar fae, Ritasia would call on her mother, Queen Irenis, and well, curses, Serena would be done for. This was not at all how she had planned this.

Ritasia hadn't spied Serena yet, thank the goddess. But she was tracking his faery dust trail to the beach–ware shop and would soon see just where Serena crouched beside the sleeping fae. Since Serena was visible to humans, she couldn't just blink out and vanish. Not unless no one was watching. Since the two men were still studying her, she couldn't use fae travel in front of them.

Dash it all anyway. She scrambled to her feet and instantly caught Ritasia's eye. Oh well, it was sure to happen. The fae's dark eyes widened. Yep, no winged fae would be caught dead on Denkar-claimed territory.

Nor would they knock out a Denkar, royal or otherwise, without paying the consequences. She smiled a little.

Princess Ritasia's gaze quickly shifted to the sleeping fae, and Serena imagined that the man was Niall, the one who Ritasia was searching for. The woman's mouth dropped open.

Time to make a hasty retreat.

Serena stalked off to the edge of the building, whipped around it, and intended to vanish, but a whole group of teens wearing shorts and T–shirts were standing there talking. They gaped at her. The wings made people do that sometimes. She usually only appeared at Renaissance fairs where lots of humans ran around dressed as faux fairies wearing fur tails—who knew why—although she speculated some were going for an elf look. Though she was fairly certain no self–

respecting elf would wear furry tails either. Must have been the humans' fanciful notions.

She loved to trick–or–treat for goodies at Halloween, wearing her wings. Woe to the human who wouldn't give her some really good treats—chocolates were her favorite. No pennies. No hard, sticky candy. Chocolates. The rich dark variety. Milk chocolate was pretty good, too. And mint chocolate, her absolute favorite.

And no apples. Whoever heard of eating anything healthy for Halloween? It was a time to be decadent.

One of the male teens drew close, staring at Serena's wings. "Wow, those are too cool. They look real." She could see in his fascinated expression that he wanted to feel one of her wings. He reached out to touch one.

She tried to couch her anger so that the golden ring didn't glow around her eyes, a sure way to tell a fae was pissed. "Hands off, buster," she quickly said, sidestepping his grasping fingers.

It wasn't like he could hurt her wings or anything. But it was just too...*personal*. It would be like him trying to kiss her, or stroking her arm, when she didn't even know the dude.

"Back off," she said, when one of the other males crowded her.

"What's wrong? Think you're too good for us?"

Oh, yeah, she did. But she was more concerned about getting out of everyone's sight so she could vanish before Ritasia called for the royal guard and Serena was clamped in faery irons—the special kind that prevented fae travel.

She tried to move around the teens, but they encircled her, touching her wings, ignoring her protests, and the fact that her eyes were glowing. The golden aura reflected off a girl's nearly black eyes as she stared open mouthed at Serena's eyes.

"Wow, look at the contacts she's wearing. Where did you get those? I gotta have me some of those. Take them out. Let me see them," the girl said.

The humans were ordering her about? A royal fae? She was supposed to play with them, not the other way around!

Fingers traced her back where the slits of her dress fit comfortably around her wings and hid the fact that they were permanently attached to her body. At home, they normally wore backless dresses to more easily accommodate their wings. But in the human world, she couldn't chance them seeing her like that.

"So real," the guy that was touching her way too intimately said.

She wanted to use her faery dust on them and put them all to sleep, teach them to mess with one of her kind. Then she could disappear without them seeing her fae vanishing act. Yet it was already too late. She heard the sound of a troop of fae running on the pavement headed straight in her direction, though none were visible to the teens. Even *she* couldn't actually see them because of the teens surrounding her. She knew the fae would be invisible when they tried to take her into custody. And she knew that's exactly what had to be running with such determination in her direction.

She sighed, doing what she knew she shouldn't under any circumstances, but these seemed to preclude all else, and vanished.

Collective gasps from the teens rent the air as the Denkar fae guard pushed them aside and found all that was left of her was her faery dust. If a tracker was among them, they could follow her easily enough.

The hunt would be on.

Nothing had gone as planned.

CHAPTER 2

Two days later, Niall woke with the most excruciating headache, wondering what in the world had happened to him.

And then he recalled bits and pieces. He had seen the most remarkable Mabara winged fae painting on the wall in South Padre Island and meant to stop her. Now, he was lying in his mostly cloaked bed, although the curtain was open on one side, which he thought odd, until he rubbed his temple, and a woman gasped. He turned to look at who had made the feminine sound and saw a maid sitting in a chair, watching over him.

Which confused him. A maid wouldn't be sitting beside his bed, unless he'd been terribly ill, but he didn't recall having come down with any sickness.

Her eyes wide, she quickly stood, offered a hasty thanks to all the goddesses, curtseyed, and hurried out of the chamber.

She'd tell the queen and everyone he was awake, and he would be questioned mercilessly about what had happened. Which meant he had to hurry and wipe away the cobwebs of his mind, so he *could* remember what had happened to make him feel this way.

Heavy footfalls immediately headed in the direction of his chamber door. He was surprised to see the crown prince stalk into his chamber first, not a physician.

Prince Deveron entered the chamber and closed in on the bed, then stood right next to it, crossed his arms over his chest, staring down at Niall for some time, then grinned at him. "So, what happened? Exactly?"

The most intriguing female Mabara had knocked Niall out with her debilitating sleeping potion! That's what had happened!

Deveron's dark hair was windswept, and he was wearing blue jeans and a T—shirt and sneakers, meaning he'd just been human side recently. Rarely did he visit anywhere in his invisible fae form, so he always dressed right for every occasion.

"Here I expect to see my loyal count at my side later in the afternoon, but you don't return to the castle. Then Ritasia grows concerned for your welfare, although I wouldn't have bothered looking for you until you'd missed evening meal. And here she finds you sleeping beside a fae–painted wall. She sees the girl who shot you with the sleeping powder. A fae of the royal house of Mabara. Who left a cryptic message for the Denkar. Care to explain?" Deveron continued.

Niall closed his eyes and groaned, his head splitting in two. "Later."

"No, not later," Deveron said. "*Now*. I will go easier on you than my mother. So, consider this practice for the real inquisition. She hasn't been home to hear of this news and no one will send word to her because you know what a terror she can be when angered. Not only did the osprey fae enter our territory, leave a message on our wall, but she put one of the members of our royal house in a sleep–induced state for two days, and she managed to elude our trackers for all that time."

Niall groaned again. Every word the prince spoke grated on his nerves. He might have slept for two days straight, but he felt he could sleep for another whole year and still need more rest.

"Niall!" Deveron snapped. "Come, come. My sister said she was quite beautiful, this winged fae. So, tell me, what did she look like?"

"The devil," Niall ground out.

Deveron smiled. "Have a hangover, do we?" Then he frowned. "Serves you right for not warning us the winged elf was wreaking havoc in our domain and not seeking help in apprehending her." Deveron let out his breath. "My mother will be furious. What can you tell me about the girl?"

When Niall didn't say a word, though he almost smiled at Deveron's reference to the girl being a mischievous winged elf, Deveron continued, "Ritasia was so shocked to see her, and then to find that she'd knocked you out with one of her toxins, she didn't get enough of a look at her. Except to say she was beautiful."

Niall let out his breath on a heavy sigh. "She's of the Mabara royal house." His voice sounded groggy and not half as irritated as he meant to sound.

"Yes, yes, this we know. And? What else?"

"My lord…"

"*And*…?" Deveron insisted. "If you aren't going to abide by protocol, which means calling for reinforcements when in a situation like you found yourself, you have no one to blame but yourself."

Niall gave an exasperated sigh this time. "She was beautiful. Blonde, green–eyed, pixie–like, and her wings were black-lined windowpanes. She wore a short black dress, grayish stockings, and pink…ballerina shoes."

Deveron raised his brows. "*And?*"

"She carries a blow–dart gun in a pocket hidden in her dress."

"You know they often have them on their person."

"I…" Niall rubbed his eyes. "I didn't think she had any way to conceal such a weapon."

"Ahh. So, you tried to apprehend her."

"Aye."

"And?"

Niall made a disgruntled face at his prince, who gave him a smug smile back.

"She shot me with a face full of her faery dust— sleeping variety. Thank the gods it wasn't the deadly kind."

Deveron's expression turned serious again. "Now, she's a wanted fae. Not only did she leave some kind of message on our wall, but she did it in broad daylight with her wings on full display, she shot one of our royal kind, *and* she vanished in front of a group of teens."

Niall closed his gaping mouth. "No."

"Indeed. Of course, my mother will want her imprisoned for what she has done, and most likely her own people will want her locked away for a very long time in some castle tower for the same reason." Deveron frowned again. "She's of a royal house, which means she could be a duchess or countess, or any number of cousins related to those of the main royal house. Did you ask her name?"

Ask her name? Niall rolled his eyes. At least he thought he did. His head hurt to such a degree, he wasn't certain if he did it properly.

Deveron twisted his mouth in derision. "Why have you, *of all people*, picked up that annoyingly human expression? Even Ritasia has started copying Alicia's way of rolling her eyes. At least Alicia lived among the humans, so she had a reason to pick up the human mannerism, but…" The prince let his observation trail off with a dark look meant to make his point.

Niall grimaced. If he could have rolled his eyes again without hurting his head, he would have.

Deveron frowned. "Our trackers are still searching for her. The trail seems to have grown cold. A spy has infiltrated the Mabara house. They are in an uproar. But since our spy was serving as a traveling bard and is not a member of the royal household, no one would tell him anything. A maid did say a young woman had left the palace and hadn't returned. When he asked which woman, she wouldn't say. Which makes me think she's one of the more important women of the household. And the royal family doesn't want anyone else to know the woman may be roaming alone in any of the other kingdoms making her an easy target to take hostage."

Niall grunted. He didn't think she was in the least bit easy to take hostage. "She would be hard to miss because of her remarkable wings."

"Remarkable?" Deveron asked. "Hmm. Did you...were you...able to gain her confidence in any way?"

Niall opened his mouth to speak, then clamped his lips shut. How could the prince even come up with such a conclusion when the woman had poisoned him with a sleeping potion that was making him feel so out of sorts? Not that the prince's questioning didn't have something to do with the way he was feeling.

Deveron cleared his throat. "Anything you can recall might be helpful."

A decidedly wicked gleam of pleasure shown in Deveron's dark eyes. What was he getting at? Niall could barely concentrate on much of anything. If the prince wanted him to tell him something, he needed to make his request clearer.

Deveron finally shrugged. "Did you kiss her?"

"Did I kiss *who*?" Niall asked the crown prince, his voice rising in irritation. He thought maybe the drug had affected his thoughts because surely Deveron couldn't have asked him such an inane question about the winged fae. Niall kissed lots of lion fae, but Deveron already knew that, and he couldn't have had that thought in mind when he asked the question.

Again, Deveron's mouth curved up in a smug smile. "We thought that's maybe why she only paralyzed you. Well, knocked you out because you'd kissed her, but didn't kill you because she somewhat liked your kiss."

Niall frowned at him. "Why would I kiss an osprey fae who was painting graffiti on one of *our* walls?"

"You kiss all kinds of fae."

"Only of the Denkar kind."

"And she was beautiful."

"She was trespassing."

Deveron didn't say anything, but he looked too amused.

"All right, so why do you think I kissed her?"

"You were wearing a fae's shimmering pink lip gloss on your lips—the only kind that can be seen when the lights are out, sparkling like shiny sprinkles of faery dust—a sure sign that you had kissed a female fae. No Denkar fae would admit that you had kissed one of them before your untimely drugged state, so we have to assume you kissed the winged fae."

Niall closed his gaping mouth. Goddess above, he'd thought he'd only dreamed the winged creature had kissed him. He barely remembered her lips pressed against his, serious, too. As if she was making a point. Not soliciting his response. Soft, warm, and—

"Well?" Deveron asked.

Irritated, Niall scowled at Deveron, hating that he'd hound him in this way. He wanted to recall more of the kiss, now that he realized it had been real, not a figment of his dream-filled imagination. But he couldn't recall anything further if Deveron continued to question him. Why couldn't he let it go?

However, Niall had to set the prince straight. "I…*didn't* kiss her."

Not that he wouldn't have wanted to kiss her back if he'd had the strength. If she'd wanted him to. Or, even if she hadn't. It was her fault for being in their territory without permission. And for kissing him when he couldn't respond in kind.

But the winged fae's kissing Niall put a whole different light on the situation. Why would she have kissed him? Because she felt sorry for having knocked him out? Or was it a case of her attempting to make him look foolish with his own kind? He didn't feel foolish in the least, but more than intrigued.

With a devilish look as if he knew better, Deveron smiled. "Sorry to say that no one will believe you. The rumors have already spread to the sphinx and turtle fae kingdoms by now. You were trying to kiss the winged fae, managed a good deal, too—as evidenced by how much lip gloss you were wearing, so it wasn't a really brief, barely–there peck on the lips—and she shot you with sleeping dust. Good thing she wasn't carrying around the more lethal dust. Although, knowing their kind, she probably had it concealed in another hidden pocket. Maybe she even got the two mixed up and meant to use the other." Again, Deveron smiled.

Niall couldn't believe the tales that were spinning wildly through the kingdoms over the mischievous fae's actions. That brought a new thought to mind, not one that he liked at all. Maybe she did this just to prove to him that she'd had the situation well in hand. Which meant, he had been powerless to prove he was in control. And by kissing him, she'd let the whole fae world that might learn of it, know so. *Devious fae*. She had sealed his fate. It would take forever to live this down.

His head pounding with frustration, Niall scowled. "*She* kissed *me*, not the other way around."

At once, he regretted his words. It sounded as though she'd had him under her power. He certainly hadn't been in any shape to take advantage of the situation. But *he* was the dark fae in his *own* territory and *should* have been the one in charge!

The smile disappeared from Deveron's face. "Really?" Then he grinned. "The story gets better and better. Sleep, Niall. My mother will be a terror when she returns and questions you. Best if you're well rested before that happens."

"Did you…did you decipher what she was trying to say?"

TERRY SPEAR

"It's in a language none of us have seen before. Our educators are searching the books for clues as we speak."

***

Never in a millennium would the Denkar suspect Serena would return to the scene of her crime as she invisibly watched through a beachfront store window across the street as five scholarly-looking fae dressed in their royal blue robes, studied her graffiti-covered wall. She had changed into her royal fae gowns of pale blue silk and matching ballet-like shoes, since no humans would see her this time.

What were the dark fae scholars doing? The message was perfectly clear.

But the way they scratched their heads and conversed with one another for so long made her think they didn't know what she'd said.

Like her, they were invisible to the humans and had already had to deal with a couple of human painters wearing white jeans and T-shirts who had tried to whitewash the concrete block wall. Before one of the painters could climb a ladder to reach the top of the wall, one of the Denkar toppled it. Another knocked over one of the opened cans, splattering the white paint all over the sidewalk.

She smiled, thinking she'd have done the same thing in their place to stop the humans from painting over her message.

Both men cursed almost as good as a pissed-off fae could, but they looked unsettled, too. Which was the fae's whole purpose in messing with them as if they were a ghostly presence to be reckoned with. They would force the humans to leave the wall alone, one way or another.

The fae could have photographed the wall, but they normally didn't use human cameras to take pictures of objects or subjects. They lived too long to be bothered with saving hundreds of thousands of pictures that they could take over the years, and what would they need with photo albums? Or why would they gather about on Facebook and show off their photos? Although many were on Facebook to play tricks on the humans. They borrowed pictures they loved to use as their own, too, when they felt moved to do so.

But the fae lived for today and for tomorrow. So, no sense in keeping pictures of the past.

Besides, physically observing the actual wall might give the Denkar clues they'd otherwise miss. For one, they couldn't see Serena's dust trail in a photo.

She studied the wall and wondered if she'd used the wrong fae language in the message. She was always mixing up the symbols in the languages, which was probably due to trying to study too many at the same time, even a couple of them that were considered dead languages since the fae who had used them no longer existed. She was the only one in the family that even attempted to learn the other written languages, finding them fascinating. Her kind thought the rest of the writings were inferior to their own, so why try to learn anyone else's? But if she was to play with the other fae, she wanted to leave a message in their own language.

Only, she guessed this time the game was on her.

Fine. She'd try it again. Different wall, different spot near the beach. And this time she'd write it out on a piece of paper beforehand to ensure she got it right, then transfer the message to the wall.

Bringing her attention back to the store Serena was standing in as she watched out the big picture window, she heard a clerk say to a woman trying on a beach dress near the dressing rooms, "Oh, yes, that looks just lovely on you."

Serena turned around to see what looked so lovely on the woman and stared at the ugly monstrosity—the dress, not the customer. Although anyone wearing the dress would instantly look nearly as awful—the gauche colors, the hideous billowing sack, the ragged edging on the sleeves and hem of the dress as if the seamstress had forgotten to hem it.

Her faeness coming to the forefront, like a ventriloquist, Serena threw her voice, making it sound close to the clerk as if she was the one speaking again and said, "That is the most hideous-looking dress in the store. The color makes your skin look splotchy and sallow. The style, if it could be said to have any style at all, adds a hundred pounds onto your weight."

If that didn't do it, nothing would discourage the woman from buying the dress. Yet, Serena loved the gaping look on the customer's face, and on the store clerk's, too, and couldn't leave well enough alone. Although if she'd been truly in a mischievous mood, she would have encouraged the woman to buy the goddess-awful dress.

"Not only that, but it looks like something you dragged out of a rag bag. The colors clash in such a horrible fashion that they wouldn't look good on anyone, no matter—"

A hand seized Serena's shoulder, and she was so startled, she shrieked.

CHAPTER 3

"She's in the dungeon, clamped in fae irons so she cannot use fae travel to escape," Deveron informed Niall, who still didn't have all his wits about him as he rested in his bed only half awake.

The last time Niall had felt this bad, he'd been drinking tequila at one of the lounges in South Padre Island and had lost count of the number of drinks he'd managed to get down while flirting with a human girl. *Big mistake*. The girl had laughed at him, not with him, and he'd suffered a hangover the size of the Denkar's kingdom. He had *never* planned to repeat that folly.

He stared groggily at the crown prince, who was wearing a black tunic and breeches, his golden medallion on full display, a warning to whoever he met that he was serving in his lion fae princely role.

"What?" Niall asked, not comprehending the matter at all.

"*The winged fae.* Come, come, Niall, snap out of it! You've had another half a day to sleep and though several of our people have questioned the girl, none can get a word out of her."

The winged fae was in the dungeon?

Deveron continued speaking as if Niall fully understood everything he said. "Since she kissed you, maybe you can wheedle something out of the pixie."

Not likely. Niall truly believed the fae had kissed him to mark him, to further humiliate him, knowing her lip gloss left shimmering fae sparkles on his mouth, which would reveal all. Unless of course he'd said *he* was the one to have kissed the girl, then let her deny that! If he hadn't been so out of it when Deveron had questioned him earlier, Niall might have done just that.

But it was too late for making up tales.

Deveron folded his arms, looking as imperious as always. "You were right though. She is beautiful in an impish sort of way. Oh, and by the way, hidden in the gowns she wore today, she did have the toxic powder hidden in another pocket. I imagine she had both with her the last time. I truly do wonder if she meant to use that on you and not the other."

How could the prince believe *that* when the girl had kissed Niall? Then he saw the gleam in Deveron's eye and knew in his dark way, he was teasing him.

"Do get dressed and I'll see you shortly below stairs."

Deveron stalked out of the room and one of Niall's

manservants entered. "May I help you dress, my lord?"

Niall scowled. He needed to sleep! Not get dressed. Not speak with the fae. After what she'd put him through, he wanted to strangle her! If he could only summon the strength to get out of bed.

Feeling like he'd been run over by a fae cavalry, he finally managed to dress and tried to look like he was walking with fierce purpose and determination, even though he thought he might be listing to one side a little. He didn't think his stride was quite as intimidating as it usually was. At least the way the servants peered at him with concerned expressions made him think so. One or two of them looked like they wanted to reach out to steady him, but when he scowled fiercely at them, they quickly kept to themselves.

He was not in the need of assistance or coddling.

By the time he'd made his way down the massive marble steps to the main floor, he was ready to grab the nearest satin–covered lounger and collapse. Sweat beaded on his brow from the exertion, and more concerned courtiers watched his every step as if afraid he'd falter at any moment.

All because of one winged fae! Payback was hell. He'd make sure of it. *If* he could stay awake long enough.

When he finally had managed the narrow winding stairs into the dank dungeon, the smell of creosol torches and musty damp air assaulted him. Served her right to be stuck here in one of the cells.

He hadn't had the need to come down here in eons,

and he was glad for it.

He noticed four Denkar fae prisoners lounging on their cots in the separate austerely furnished cells, all male. Female fae, although cunning and devious, usually were more subtle in their pranks and didn't get incarcerated as often.

Each of the men looked him over, sure to wonder what Niall was doing down here.

The males in the cells had committed various infractions from the theft of ancient artifacts at one of the digs in their kingdom, to disobeying the queen's ruling on making mischief in one of the Denkar's related minor kingdoms. Some fae thought if they were members of the major kingdom, they could get away with pulling shenanigans on the fae of the minor kingdoms. Although it depended on the time of year, just like some humans celebrated April Fool's Day or All Fool's Day. Even the Romans had celebrated such a day known as Hilaria and in medieval times in Spanish–speaking countries, the Festival of Fools. The fae kind had set a couple of days aside for tomfoolery as well. As long as the trickery wasn't too severe, then no problem existed.

Niall recalled the history lessons concerning the fun-loving fae from the various kingdoms, who had descended on the human populations all over the world in ancient times, to begin the All Fool's Day tradition. One of his favorite lessons was concerning the trickery that a fae concocted whereby several humans arrived at the Tower of London to observe the lions being washed.

Or the one where the Swiss had learned of a way to eliminate the dreaded spaghetti weevil and were producing a bumper crop from spaghetti trees.

That was the way of the fae after all. To encourage the most outrageous of fool-worthy pranks and see just how many humans fell for them.

So, hoaxes such as those wouldn't have received a second notice in the fae kingdoms.

But one of the jailed Denkar had stolen a turtle fae's bride right before she walked down the aisle to the altar, which would have been acceptable if the bride had agreed, but she hadn't. Since the girl was a distant cousin of Prince Deveron's, the queen had been incensed.

One of the incarcerated fae had tried to steal a kiss from Princess Ritasia, Prince Deveron's sister—whether she had encouraged it or not—when the queen had no intention of his seeking her daughter's hand in marriage!

The last confined male fae had made the grievous mistake of saying that Queen Irenis's dark and fathomless eyes didn't inspire terror like the cobra fae queen's did. Whether Queen Irenis's eyes did or not was mere speculation. But saying such a thing landed the fae in a cell for his impudence. Which made the point: her subjects could believe anything they wanted, but they'd better keep their thoughts to themselves if the queen should take offense.

As soon as Niall made it to the very last cell for prisoners deemed warranting special treatment, isolated from the other cells by stone walls and a metal door with only a barred window that guards and the like could look into, he was surprised to see Deveron and five other fae in attendance.

He had mistakenly assumed, since he was needed because of his special *connection* to the girl, that he'd have a private audience with the winged fae. Maybe the Denkar thought the girl would try to kiss Niall and convince him to release her if they left him alone with her. As much as his head was pounding, he silently scoffed at that.

He meant to stand erect next to Deveron, scowling fiercely, intimidatingly like all the rest of his kind looked, but by the gods, he could barely stand!

Teetering and forcing himself not to lean against Deveron's solid form, Niall frowned even more at the winged fae.

She should have appeared afraid, as darkly dangerous as his kind looked. They were hunters, after all. And appeared damn displeased. But the nerve of the creature!

She was lying on her back, wrists manacled, her hands beneath her head, legs crossed at the ankles, wearing long silk gowns of pale blue of a fashion suited to fae royalty, and looking more alluring than he was willing to admit, as she stared up at the ceiling with a contemplative expression even. She didn't appear in the least bit scared. Which made everyone else in the room even angrier.

"Speak with her, Niall!" Deveron demanded,

sounding highly agitated.

Before Niall fell down, his head was in such a state of fuzziness, he took several steps toward the straw mattress suspended on ropes, covered in a scratchy black woolen blanket, then pushed the girl's satin slipper-covered feet aside and sat down on the edge of the bed.

He didn't want to let on that he could no longer stand. But he was certain his people would jump to their own conclusions about his action. And not in a way that would please him.

Not only did his own Denkar kind stare at him with mouths agape, except for Deveron, whose eyebrows arched heavenward also, the winged fae finally tore her gaze from the ceiling and looked at him to see who was encroaching on her space. Her eyes widened in recognition.

"Yes, it is me," he said hotly.

"You have recovered," she said softly.

He was surprised to hear the regret in her voice. What kind of a game was she playing?

"What is your name?"

"The message," Deveron said, as if her name meant nothing.

Niall cast Deveron a dark look. *Who* was doing the questioning?

Deveron gave *him* an even darker look.

Niall relented and asked the girl, "What was your message?"

She smiled and folded her arms. "If they leave, I'll

tell you."

"You will tell us now," Deveron commanded.

Someday Deveron would be king. Already he wore the royal mantle well.

"Or?" she asked.

She had the most exasperatingly impish way of speaking that would infuriate any sane person. Even so, Niall stifled a chuckle. He couldn't believe she'd speak thus to the crown prince of the Denkar fae!

"My lord," Niall said, "please give me a few minutes to speak with her alone."

Deveron studied the wench, then Niall could see he was giving in, his rigid posture relaxing marginally— only for the moment though. "Explain to her if she doesn't tell you what we wish to know, she *will* suffer the consequences."

Niall knew what that would entail. Starvation, dehydration, sleep deprivation, even torture, if they thought it was necessary. They would eventually learn what they wanted from her. But he didn't want it to go that far and would do everything in his power to convince her to speak up before it was too late.

When Deveron led the other men from the cell, Niall said again, "What is your name?"

"Serena." She smiled sweetly at him. "Come closer."

He knew the guards would have removed her weapons, so he wasn't concerned she'd put him in another comatose state. But he wasn't about to let her play him either.

"What was your message?" he asked, firmly, without hesitation, demanding an answer, not moving any closer to her.

"I'm sorry. I didn't mean to put you to sleep. You had startled me."

He snorted. Although her words sounded like the truth, he still couldn't believe she had kissed him. "Why did you kiss me?"

Her lips turned up in the most exasperatingly, wicked smile. "I give you permission to kiss me back."

He stared at her with incredulity. "I would not wish it under any circumstances."

"That's not what you indicated when I kissed you."

His mouth opened, but he clamped his lips tight after that. What had he done? Certainly not encouraged her in any way. He had been dead to the world.

Without his asking, she gave him the answer. "You smiled after I kissed you."

He arched one brow.

She shrugged. "I guess it was good for you."

In his dreams, yes. Ignoring her comment, he asked the one that Queen Irenis herself would wish answered soon. "What was the message that you'd painted on the wall?"

"Take me there, and I'll interpret it for you."

Hearing her words, he smiled.

"You are not afraid, are you?"

As if he was afraid of the girl. "You can tell me right

here what you said on the wall."

"I don't think so. I believe, if your people cannot read it, I must have written the message wrong."

"All right, then tell me what you had intended to say." When she looked downright mutinous and wouldn't say, he warned, "The queen will not go easy with you."

Despite what Serena had done to him and fighting the urge to believe her when she said she was sorry for putting him to sleep and giving him this headache to rival any other, he didn't want her harmed.

Maybe it had been the kiss she'd given him that swayed his thinking.

"If I do something for you, will you help me to escape?" she whispered.

His jaw dropped. She *had* to be kidding.

CHAPTER 4

As soon as Serena found herself in irons in a lion fae cell, she knew she was in real trouble. But she'd put on airs that none of this mattered to her in the least. She wouldn't beg Niall, although if he didn't agree to rescue her, she was considering doing just that.

"Hurry," she said, her voice hushed, knowing that most likely someone from the dark fae court hidden from her view outside the cell was trying to hear everything she and Niall talked about.

As if he was trying to humor her, Niall said in a conspiratorial whisper back, "What would you give me that would convince me to free you?" He looked as though he was fighting a smile.

But he also was so nearly out of it because of the potion she'd dosed him with, that he had to sit on the bed at her feet and looked as though he could lie down right beside her and sleep another forty hours. She had a reputation for making extremely powerful sleeping potions.

"I will eliminate any of the side effects that you suffer from because of the sleeping powder that I had blasted you with. I must warn you, the effects can last up to two months or even longer."

He sat up a little straighter, his eyes widening fractionally.

Yeah, he was interested all right.

"But the antidote I have is not with me."

He gave her a look like that figured.

She lifted her shoulder in a slight shrug. "It would not do to carry the antidote with me if others could wrest it away from me and counter the effect of the drug. So, I would have to take you with me to the place where I keep my supply."

He gave her a small smile and an even slighter shake of his head. "Next, you will have to deal with Queen Irenis herself." He rose from the bed too suddenly, and he nearly collapsed, cursed under his breath, and grabbed the bed to take his seat again.

"The antidote will remove all the effects of the drug, I swear it," she whispered, as she heard footfalls approaching the cell.

Someone else would interrogate her, and she knew he would not go easy on her. She would have to admit she was the princess before long, and all would be lost.

***

Never in a million years would Niall consider

removing a prisoner from a cell when the queen had ordered the prisoner put there. *Never.* But no way could he continue to feel as if he was on a drugged-out binge, unable to function properly no matter how hard he tried. For two months or longer? He couldn't deal with feeling like this for that long.

"If you are lying to me...," he said softly with a hint of dark warning. He would strangle her himself.

"I am not lying to you," she said, reaching her manacled wrists out to him.

The queen would terminate him herself if she knew what he was now considering on doing, but he couldn't live like this either. He only hoped he could convince his aunt someday that he had no choice but to do what he was about to do. He headed for the wrought iron hook that held the key to the manacles and the cell.

He rushed back to the bed with the key to the manacles in hand. "They will be listening."

"The message states that I wish the queen well on her birthday," Serena said for all to hear.

Niall looked up from the manacles he was unlocking to see Serena's expression. She was smiling.

He let out his breath, pulled the manacles away, but not before he seized one of her wrists. If she fae traveled, she was taking him with her.

Footfalls reached the door, and the bolt was thrown open.

The winged fae vanished in the way of fae travel, only this time taking Niall with her just as he heard

Deveron shout, "No! Niall!"

Niall knew he'd be manacled in that cell next as soon as the trackers caught up with him. But he could handle anything if Serena would give him the antidote.

When they alighted, they were behind a shell of a building as if it was one of those movie props Niall had heard of. Behind him was a wall of trees, and he wondered where Serena had taken him.

He was glad he was used to fae travel or he would have been dizzy from transporting in that way. As bad as he felt from her drug, he probably would have been on his knees when he arrived. Which would not have mattered due to the way he was feeling, but he did not want to look that indisposed in front of the winged fae.

He glanced around again, smelling turkey legs roasting and a hint of smoke on the hot humid breeze. Where in the world were they?

The most exquisite Russian-sounding gypsy music played in the distance as a man shouted, "Come ye, folk, see what wares I have to offer ye."

Was this a village in Mabara?

"Where is the cure?" Niall asked, not letting go of Serena's wrist in the event she attempted to fae travel again. *Without him this time.*

She sighed and with a hard twist of her wrist, broke free of him. Before he could grab her wrist again, she took his hand as if they were boyfriend and girlfriend on a stroll in a park. Feeling her warm hand around his, he stared at her incredulously. Did she really like him? Or was this just a ploy to give him a false sense of security to make him believe she didn't intend to run out on him?

"At least since you are wearing your tunic, breeches, and high leather suede boots, you'll fit in nicely here," she said cheerfully.

Why wouldn't he fit in? He was wearing the height of fashion for any royal in any of the kingdoms. Not that he was that fashion conscious, but Queen Irenis expected it of any royals in her kingdom. When they visited the human world, they could dress as sloppy as the humans—to fit in. So, while he was at South Padre Island, he loved to wear a pair of torn jeans, scuzzy sneakers, and a thousand–times washed T-shirt that was so soft, he barely felt it against his skin.

But he had business to take care of, and it had nothing to do with how he was dressed or what her hand on his was doing to his hormones and the fascination she held for him.

"Where is the antidote?" he asked again, growling this time as she steered him around the back of the building, and they began to walk down a treed path where tons of people dressed in the strangest attire clustered in groups on either side or walked in front of them or toward them in a hurry to get somewhere.

The first thing he noticed was that they were all humans dressed in royal 19th Century clothing, or earlier periods. Highlanders in kilts, a Native American in buckskins, men and women dressed in leathers featuring silver chains and other silver ornaments that glistened in the sunlight—though he wasn't sure what the people dressed in such a fashion were supposed to be.

And nearby, stalls for selling food: turkey legs, ice cream, sandwiches, and shops offering the strange clothing the humans were wearing, hats from varying centuries, copper dragon fountains spouting water, and pewter dragons curled around crystal balls in another. He'd never seen anything so strange like this place.

He noticed then a couple of men with a faint fae aura, but they quickly disappeared into a tavern where the sign read, "Ale Served Here."

Ale. He wouldn't touch a drop as bad as *he* was feeling. "Where in the world are we?"

"A Renaissance fair in north Texas. The humans love fairs as much as we do. Look at all the winged fairies," she said, motioning to women dressed in the craziest garb of shimmering, silky, colorful creations. Wings were attached to their garments, while long furry tails swung behind them as the women swayed their hips.

Fur tails?

Several of the pretend winged fairies nodded to her in greeting as if Serena was one of them.

He shook his head, guessing she must come here often, but he shifted his attention to the reason he'd let her out of the dungeon in the first place. *"Where...do...you...have...the...cure?"*

"Oh, it is not here," she said, her expression serious now. "You know as well as I do, your people will be looking for us as soon as they get their trackers on our fae dust trails. I cannot disguise mine. And I'm sure if you could hide yours, you wouldn't. So, I couldn't take you directly to where my antidote is hidden. My people could never let yours get their hands on the cure. I wish only to give it to you."

He understood her need to deter the trackers. But it wasn't helping his condition any. Yet again, he wondered if her willingness to help him hid some secret agenda. Why else would she offer to undo what she had done to him?

Unless she truly did like him. To a degree.

"Where do we go now?" Niall frowned as the tiredness continued to plague his every step. "You know how badly I feel." Or maybe she didn't. He doubted she'd ever had to experience such a thing.

As if she could read his mind, she looked up and said, "Yes, I know exactly how you are feeling."

He raised his brows as he looked down at her, unable to believe she would. Unless...

"I tried to use the powder on a thief once." She shrugged. "That day it was just one mistake of a whole mess of them I'd made. First, I shouldn't have been alone."

"Like you were on South Padre Island," he scolded. Even if she hadn't been painting on their wall, he didn't like the idea she was a female fae running around on her own with no one to watch out for her. Why wasn't anyone in better charge of her? She was a royal after all.

She let out her breath. "I was only eight, so it was

really foolish of me to stray so far from the castle. You see, I was practicing with my powder, pulling my pipe out of my pouch as quickly as I could, blowing on it with just a hint of pressure so that I could ensure I sent only a measured amount to its destination each time. It's important to practice, you know. So, I was getting ready to blow again, when I heard footfalls behind me.

"I turned and saw a large man grinning at me, not slowing down as he ate up the ground with his hefty stride. His teeth were mottled yellow and brown, his blue eyes hard with speculation. I wasn't sure what he intended, but as soon as he drew close, I blew the powder at him. Only the breeze was such that it tossed it all back into my face. He was chuckling as he watched me fall."

Niall tightened his free hand into a fist, wanting to protect the winged child that had been at the mercy of such a brute. "And?"

She gave a bitter laugh. "Here I am, a fae with the power to harness the wind and I hadn't remembered the direction the breeze was blowing because I was concentrating on the distance the man was to me. If I had been thinking more clearly, I could have used my ability to toss the powder right back at him. Easily."

"You were only a child," Niall said, caustically, not angry with Serena, but at any who might have harmed her. "What happened?"

"He stole everything I had and left me sleeping there. My mother's royal guard found me. If I hadn't been so out of it when I finally came to, I'm certain she would have lectured me more. She had even contemplated not giving me the antidote. For my own good, she said. A lesson learned sort of thing."

Niall frowned at the notion.

"But she decided I'd been terrified enough. I never left the castle again without a guard."

He snorted at that.

"Not until I was thirteen. By then I had become much more skilled in the way of harnessing the wind and controlling the dispersing of sleeping powders and the like."

This time he humpfed.

She cast him an irritated look.

He looked down at her. "You are still getting into trouble on your own."

She smiled up at him and the look was pure imp.

But then he felt the tiredness return, and a shop selling hammocks caught his eye. Blue and red and green hammocks hung from the porch roof, offered for sale where two clunky humans reclined, dressed as court jesters in black and white harlequin satiny fabric. Niall gazed longingly at the comfortable looking hanging beds made of canvas.

Niall was dying to try out one of the hammocks, even if it meant tipping it over and dumping the current occupant on the wooden porch. Niall would have to become invisible first, upend one of the hammocks, and then return in his visible form to the shop. The other jester would have a good laugh at the expense of the one sitting on the porch, who would be trying to figure out what had happened. It seemed an appropriate situation for a pair of jesters, aye?

He noticed then, Serena was motioning with her hand every once in a while, and though he thought she had been waving at other faux fairies, he realized a surge of a breeze carried his and her unique fae dust trails off into the woods with every wave of her hand.

So, she might not be able to hide their trails, but she could scatter them to a degree, using her air elemental powers. Which suited him fine. He didn't want the dark fae guards to track them down before he was cured.

"Serena!" a man said, wearing a knight's silver chainmail, a black tunic covering the mail, a red lion emblazoned across the front of it as he spied her and the man who was holding hands with her. A sheathed sword hung at his side. He gave Niall a dark look that could kill.

"The Black Knight," Serena said to Niall. "He's the bad guy who fights the king's champion in the jousts."

"He's a fae," Niall said, scowling, seeing the knight's fae aura at once. "Who is he? He's not one of your kind." Which meant she shouldn't have been so friendly with him. Unless he was old enough to conceal his wings, and he was a winged fae after all. He could have been her older brother, for all Niall knew.

But then Niall studied the knight stalking toward them further, the hard jaw, the turned down mouth, the narrowed, nearly midnight blue eyes. His dusty blond hair was pulled into a knot at the top of his head, and his skin was tan. The sun glinted off his gold medallion with the fighting dragon on it—signature of the dragon fae royalty, and then Niall knew the truth. He was one of the dragon fae! *Not* Serena's brother.

Why was he jousting in a human event though?

Serena squeezed Niall's hand and smiled at the knight as he approached them.

"This is Sir Reginald of the dragon fae," she said in introduction.

The lion fae and dragon fae had been at odds for centuries, though circumstances in that regard might be changing. But still, Niall suspected, or maybe it was wishful thinking, Serena shouldn't have known the dragon fae. Not when she was of the royal house of Mabara, alone, without anyone's supervision from her castle.

"A sword instead of a bow?" Niall asked the dragon fae, a barbed jab at the man's skills. The dragon fae were known to be expert with the bow. He'd never heard of one who used a sword exclusively instead.

Niall let loose of Serena's hand and slipped his arm around her waist, pulling her snug against his side. He did so, he told himself, because he was protecting the lady from the unscrupulous dragon fae. Her people would appreciate that Niall was taking good care of her while in the company of the knight. Niall's own queen would commend him for taking the lady well in hand, for her protection, of course.

For another thing, he well outranked the man.

Serena glanced at Niall and the way he held her so close. Her heartbeat quickened, and her eyes were wide with surprise. She parted her lips as if to say something, but didn't, then quickly looked back at the knight to see his reaction to Niall's action and question. But Niall noted she did not make *any* attempt to pull away from him. And he self-contentedly smiled at that.

The knight's eyes narrowed. "We had an agreement, you and I," he said to Serena, his voice cutting. Niall could tell Reginald didn't like him touching Serena in so familiar a way. But the knight had no business wanting the lady when Niall was certain her mother knew nothing about her dalliance with the dragon fae.

She sighed. "It didn't go as intended, Reginald. You know how I sometimes mix up my languages. It seems the Denkar were not able to decipher my message."

He glowered at Niall. "Who is *he* then?"

"Count Niall of the Denkar."

The knight put his hand on the hilt of his sword.

"No," Serena warned. "He's unarmed, Reginald. He freed me from the Denkar prison."

The knight's mouth gaped. "You were imprisoned?" Then he frowned again. "Why would he free you?" Before she could respond as if he really didn't like what he might hear and said in a commanding way, "You are to be mine."

"That remains to be seen," Serena said, her back rigid. She apparently didn't like the knight's underhanded comments any more than Niall did.

"Unless the queen agrees to release me from my mother's vow to her, we can do nothing."

Niall noted she did not tell the knight why he had freed her.

"Then what is one of the Denkar doing here with you?" The knight motioned to the way Niall held her possessively.

Niall didn't know what made him say it, except that he had the greatest urge to rile the knight further, and it was the first thought that came to mind, as he asked Serena, "Have you kissed him also?"

***

Deveron was in the middle of securing two trackers to locate Niall and the winged fae named Serena when his mother sent a messenger to him, requesting his presence in her throne room. *At once.*

Just as he had expected, she would be in a dreadful mood. Only he hadn't thought this would be the reason.

"Deveron," she snapped, her dark eyes ringed with gold, as she wore bright red silk gowns, warning all in not so subtle a manner that she was in a furor over something.

She motioned for the courtiers who were standing about to leave at once. Her advisor stood planted by her side as though he thought he was needed, but when his mother gave Deveron the dark look she did now, he knew this was for his ears only.

"Out," she told her advisor, and the gray-haired Lord Haverton quickly bowed and exited the throne room, the guards shutting the doors immediately.

Deveron began to explain. "The winged fae was apprehended and taken to the dungeon where she was interrogated, but—"

His mother waved her hand dismissively. "I know all that goes on in my kingdom," she said hotly.

"I was about to send two trackers to run them down."

"Do you know who she is?" his mother asked, her brows arched with the question.

Deveron was getting a very bad feeling about this. "A royal winged fae from Mabara."

"The queen's own daughter!" his mother exclaimed with irritation.

Deveron let out his breath and folded his arms across his chest. So, he was in trouble for imprisoning the pixie-like fae. "What do you wish for me to do, my lady mother? I will not marry the girl. I fully intend to marry Alicia. You know I have my mind set on this."

The queen shook her head and tsked. "I do not intend to wed you to every princess who is eligible. Serena is to wed your cousin, Micala. The alliance will do us good."

Deveron stared at his mother, wondering when this had come about. Would she never let any of them know what she intended before she made the arrangements herself? "Does Micala know about this?"

His cousin *hadn't* any plans to settle down any time soon. And Deveron knew if his mother had spoken to

Micala concerning this, he would have told Deveron the news right away and not been happy about it.

"Of course not. I just made arrangements with the queen a few days ago and have been celebrating with her ever since."

So that's where she'd been…and why.

Thinking he might get Micala out of the bind he was in and fix Niall for freeing the winged fae and possibly getting Deveron into hot water for it at the same time, he said, "But she's kissed Niall, my lady mother, and must have some fondness for him. And now he has freed her from our dungeon. So he must return the interest. Think you he would be a better match for the winged creature?"

"Nay," his mother said, waving her hand in dismissal. "The agreement has been signed. The princess will marry Micala and that will be the last of it. Send off the trackers, and tell them…" She paused and frowned. "Did she not tell you that she was the princess?"

"No, nor would she tell us her name." Not that Deveron had asked her, only having questioned Niall when he was in bed half asleep. But Niall hadn't known her name either.

Although when Niall had tried to learn of her name in the dungeon, Deveron had stopped him from doing so. He'd only thought she was some minor royalty and it didn't matter who she truly was at that point. Who would have thought the princess herself would have being painting graffiti on their wall? All he thought important was that they learn what message she'd painted there. He reminded himself that this was one of those little life experiences to learn from. In the future, he would be more careful to discover who he was dealing with before he made the wrong assumptions.

"Be sure that Niall learns who the woman is before he becomes too interested in her," his mother warned.

"He wanted to strangle her after what she did to him," Deveron admitted.

His mother smiled at that, then scowled. "He should have known not to approach her without backup."

"Aye, as I have told him."

"Go," she said in way of releasing him from his meeting with her. "Find them before her mother learns what has become of her."

He stalked toward the door, paused, turned, and asked, "Did the princess know what her mother had intended with regard to Serena marrying Micala?"

"Of course."

"Was she pleased?"

"Of course not. Such is the task we mothers have to face. Ungrateful children who do not know enough about the politics of running kingdoms and the importance of alliances." She gave Deveron a pointed look, assuring him she included him in that category.

He didn't care as long as he didn't have to marry someone other than Alicia.

"Serena will grow to care for Micala. Now go, before her mother learns she is off with Niall, goddess knows where and what doing."

Had Serena written something discouraging about the Denkar because of the impending marriage arrangement between her and his cousin?

Great. Deveron left the throne room, motioned for three servants, and said, "Go at once to South Padre Island dressed as human painters. Under Queen Irenis's orders, paint the wall that the winged fae illustrated with her artwork. Tell the scholars who are trying to decipher it that there's no need to learn what the message said."

"Aye, my lord."

The three men hurried off while Deveron returned to the two trackers. "I'm going with you. More is at stake than I ever thought possible."

He'd kill Niall himself if he strangled the girl before he knew who she was and ultimately caused a war between their kingdoms.

CHAPTER 5

While the music from the Renaissance fair continued to serenade them, and tons of humans in their strange costumes passed them by, Sir Reginald glowered at Serena, then at Niall. "You lie. She would never have kissed the likes of you. She abhors the idea of marrying a lion fae."

Niall glanced at Serena, who looked horrified that he'd even mentioned she had kissed him, which made him smile. If her concern was because he had told on her, it served her right for kissing Niall without his being able to respond. But he also wondered about the knight's remark that Serena hated the idea of marrying one of his kind. Why would that even be an issue that she would consider?

"I challenge you to a joust," Sir Reginald told Niall.

"No! You cannot!" Serena said angrily. "He's still under the influence of my sleeping potion. You have no reason to challenge him anyway."

The knight stiffened. "Why had you put him to sleep? You wouldn't have done so *unless* he'd threatened you."

"He startled me when I was writing the message. I didn't mean to put him to sleep," she said, irritated.

The knight would not allow her to dismiss his concerns. "He would have arrested you. You said yourself you were in the lion fae dungeon."

She folded her arms and scowled at him. "You knew that might happen if one of the royal fae, and not one of their underlings, caught me writing the message. We agreed it was a risk I had to take."

A risk she had to take? For what? For this pompous aristocrat? Why didn't the knight paint the graffiti on the wall if both had agreed to do it? Why didn't *he* take the risk and not the lady? *Coward!*

Niall glowered at the man, who stood his same six-foot height and who didn't intimidate him in the least. Although the sleeping potion put Niall at a decided disadvantage. The dragon fae and the lion fae had never gotten along. And he would not let the challenge go.

"I accept," Niall said, ready to knock him off his mount at once—if he had a mount right now—just to prove to the dragon fae he had met his match. "Any man who sends a woman to do his dirty work deserves to be trounced on the playing field."

The gold rings around the knight's eyes expanded.

"No!" Serena said vehemently to Niall. "You

cannot. Not when you're still feeling the effects of the drug."

"When is the joust to be held?" Niall asked the knight, not taking his eyes off Sir Reginald, ignoring Serena's words.

"We will joust at four, in between the regularly scheduled human shows," Reginald said. "'Tis a shame we cannot play for real."

Niall knew what the knight referred to. In front of the humans, they couldn't fight to the death. But after Niall stomped the knight's honor into the dirt—worse, that he did so in front of the woman he was pursuing—he knew Reginald would want satisfaction in a permanent, deadly way.

Niall didn't hesitate to respond. "Aye. I'll be there."

"I'll wear your favor, princess," Sir Reginald said, taking her hand in his and kissing it. He didn't say it as if he genuinely wanted to wear her favor, but more that he wanted to ensure she knew he would and that she better not think of giving her favor to Niall to wear. He gave Niall one last scowl, although a shimmer of amusement glimmered in his eyes.

Niall assumed Reginald was certain he could best him, most likely because of Niall's drugged state. Which, given that, the man could be right. But he would not shirk from his duty as a lion fae.

Sir Reginald whipped around and stalked off.

"You can't fight him in the condition you're in. Can you even joust?" she asked, her voice threaded with disbelief and worry.

"I wouldn't have agreed to fight him if I didn't know how," Niall said, cross with her. He was one of the Denkar! He had trained in every form of weaponry. The only form he didn't excel at was with the bow, and there, the dragon fae nearly always had the advantage. Most seemed to be born with an uncanny ability to use the bow, although with any ability like that, training improved the skill. If they spent little practice at it, they would be no better than any other fae who trained hard at it.

But ultimately, a lion fae never backed down from a dragon fae. It just wasn't done.

Conceding that he would not let this go, Serena shook her head. "I have to get you the antidote before you fight him."

"Then let's go."

"Niall!" Deveron shouted somewhere behind them in the crowd of humans. His tone of voice sounded more worried than angry. Well, maybe a little incensed.

Niall couldn't see the prince, but he suspected Deveron was with trackers who were following their confusingly scattered fae dust trail as Serena had swept it into the woods.

"She is—" Deveron hollered.

Before he could shout anything more, Serena whisked Niall away to a field of tall wavering flowers that smelled like roses and jasmine and honeysuckle all combined.

"I don't want you fighting Sir Reginald," Serena said again, as they arrived goddess knew where.

She pulled him through the meadow filled with purple daisies, lilacs, towering hollyhocks, and broad golden sunflowers that gently swayed in the breeze. Honeysuckle covered some areas while a ground cover of fragrant jasmine clustered in others. Forests edged the meadow, and he could hear water sluicing over rocks as it made its way downriver somewhere close by. "There's no reason to do so. I'll make you well, and you can go home."

He focused on what he'd wanted to know all along. "What was the message you meant to write on the wall?"

She sighed. "The Mabara will ally with the dragon fae, not the dark fae!"

"Were you trying to start a war?" he asked incredulously, his whole body weary as he trudged along with her, hand in hand.

"Of course not. I intended a non–royal lion fae to see the message and take it back to your queen. I didn't expect to see you there. I only wanted to stop a marriage."

Niall pulled her to a halt. He had a sickening feeling about this. She wanted to marry the Black Knight, a dragon fae, but Queen Irenis had made other arrangements? She must have come to some agreement with the lady's mother. "Who were you to marry?"

"Micala."

Niall stared at her in disbelief. First, Micala wasn't

ready to settle down. Second, his cousin would have told him about an impending marriage to any fae, but especially to one who was this unusual. Third, Queen Irenis, his aunt, would not have arranged for Micala to be married to just any fae. Which set him to worrying. Had she intended to do the same for Niall without his knowledge?

So, who was Serena really?

"Who is your mother?"

She tugged her hand free, folded her arms, and gave him one of her more impudent looks. "The queen of the Mabara, Verbenia."

***

Serena knew eventually she'd have to tell Niall who she truly was, and she expected just the reaction she was getting now. Disbelief, irritation, and most likely a set determination to take her back to the dark fae kingdom to ensure she did what Queen Irenis and her mother wanted. After all, Queen Irenis was Niall's queen.

But Serena wasn't going to be forced into a marriage with a lion fae. *Period.*

Niall reached for Serena, and she stepped back, waving her arms in a manner that stated he better not touch her. "No, you won't return me to your castle. I need to give you the cure first. You'll never be able to stand a chance against the Black Knight otherwise. Isn't it your place to challenge Reginald for his trying to break up the marriage contract?"

"Nay, it isn't my place but rather it is Micala's to

challenge the knight. But since I'm certain that my cousin doesn't know about it in the first place, and you kissed me and not him, which seemed to be what made Sir Reginald so angry…"

Her face heated and she knew it had to have blossomed in color. Seeing her reaction, he smiled.

"Ha! I couldn't believe you'd tell him about it!" she said.

"Neither of you satisfied my curiosity as to what the message was all about or why he was involved," Niall said. "I thought if I brought it up, he might very well explain what it was all about." After seeing the knight's angry face, Niall probably assumed the man had never been that intimate with Serena, nor she with him. "Has he kissed you?"

"Certainly!" Which wasn't a lie.

Niall's smile broadened. "Only on the hand?"

"I'm the Mabara princess. He knows that I'd have to agree to such a thing, and so he's abiding his—"

Niall didn't even wait for her to finish what she had to say, but pulled her securely into his arms and kissed her, sweetly, tenderly, lovingly. She melted, her own senses reeling. She tentatively kissed him back, saw his eyes darkening, but he suddenly pulled away, their breaths raspy.

"Take me to where the cure is." His gaze was still on hers, but he stepped away as if he'd done something he shouldn't have. Which was true, so why was she wanting so much more?

She was still thinking about the kiss, the press of his lips on hers, the way he seemed so caring, so feeling, the way he'd enfolded her so fully in his arms. She couldn't think.

"Serena, *princess*," he said, gently, but urgently, "where have you hidden the antidote?"

"You kissed me," she said softly, touching her lips with the tip of her finger, unable to think of anything else.

"Aye. You didn't give me an opportunity to kiss you back the last time. You had me at a decided disadvantage. But it was time for me to take my turn." He gave her the most disarmingly, sweet smile.

So, it was just a way to get back at her? For having kissed him and left evidence on his lips the last time?

"He will kill you if he learns of it," Serena growled, then stalked off toward a wooded area.

"The knight?" Niall humpfed.

"I don't want you fighting him."

"You said I would have to because he was trying to stop the marriage contract between you and my cousin."

She didn't say anything,

"You really think I cannot best him?"

"Of course you cannot. He's been jousting at the fair for weeks. He loses at the very end only because that's the role he gets paid to do. But it amuses him to be the Black Knight, to hear his side cheering for him. Him, a dragon fae."

"Who is but a knight in the fae world."

Serena glowered at Niall, who was falling behind. She slowed her pace, sorry again for having drugged him. "I don't care about his rank. I'd take a knight over a count any day, if I loved him."

"Do you love him?" Niall suddenly asked, as if such a thing would even matter to him.

He was like all the rest. Whatever the queens decided would be. And if Serena didn't stop it, she'd be stuck with Micala, a count she'd never met and didn't care to meet.

"Of course I do."

But he noted her long hesitation in answering and shook his head.

"What? You don't believe me?"

"I believe you love the way he jousts. Maybe that he's going against the ruling of your queen. Probably no one else in your kingdom would think of doing such a thing. Possibly, you like that he enjoys the fair as you do. But know this, Princess, you are a conquest for him. For the dragon fae. And the king of the dragon fae would reward Reginald, if the knight could win your hand. Queen Irenis will not be appeased however. I doubt your mother will be happy either."

"If I love him…"

Niall smiled.

She stalked off. "Why would you try to stop me from marrying Reginald? I don't even know Micala. He might be an ogre!"

"He's my cousin."

She glanced back at Niall, noted his sour look, then remarked, "Well *you* don't have to marry him."

He smiled at that, then frowned. "Where are we going?"

"To gather some herbs. And you will not watch me."

"Do not tell me you have to create the potion."

She didn't say anything.

He groaned. He was falling even farther behind. When she looked back, he'd disappeared. Her heart leapt with distress. Had he fae transported? Returned to the Denkar castle to report what she was up to? To relay the message she'd written on the wall?

She raced back to where she'd seen him last and saw a separation in the tall, wavering hollyhocks and sunny sunflowers. And found him lying on the ground, his eyes shut, his arms folded across his chest.

"Are you asleep?" she whispered.

"Yes," he said, not opening his eyes. "You can kiss me again, if you like while I dream about it."

She smiled. "Then you will tell my knight, and he will challenge you again, if he doesn't kill you the first time. I'll be back as soon as I make the potion."

"Hurry," he said, but he sounded like he was already nearly asleep.

She sighed. "You will feel a strong wind, but don't worry."

"You're scattering our fae trails again."

"Yes. Sleep. I'll return as soon as I can."

He was the most honorable fae she'd ever

encountered. Except for the kiss, but that was her own fault for having kissed him first. But she'd never met a man who would challenge the knight, who would tell him just what he thought of his allowing Serena to paint the message, when Reginald knew just the kind of trouble she could get into for it. Not once had Reginald even offered to paint it instead.

And that had niggled at her to a degree.

Of course, painting the message had been her idea, so she had thought it was important that she write it. And she loved painting murals, though she hadn't done anything quite like this before. She'd had to study a lot of graffiti-covered walls in the States before she thought she had the concept down pat.

Not that the humans came up with the idea. When it came to mischief, the fae were at the root of it. She just hadn't ever painted graffiti before.

What would Niall have done in Reginald's place? Asked the queen for her hand in marriage? She wasn't sure. But she suspected he would not have allowed her to earn the queen's wrath in that manner. He'd never once acted anything but kindly toward her, even as angry as he had to be with her for drugging him. Oh sure, he'd been irritated with her, but still in a mild—mannered way—for a lion fae.

She sighed, contemplating how she could help Niall win against the knight. She would never have considered such a thing before. Aiding a lion fae warrior against a dragon fae she wished to marry?

She did wonder how Reginald would take defeat if Niall should win. That would tell her more about Reginald's true character. He always lost at the human games because he was paid to do so. He'd storm off angrily because he was supposed to. But was that his true nature?

Did she truly want to wed Sir Reginald? Or was she just trying to make a statement to her mother and to the lion fae queen? She wanted a choice! And choosing Reginald for her husband...

She glanced back at Niall. She was thinking she'd made the wrong choice. But maybe she could come up with the remedy for that, too.

Her small stone croft with its tidy thatched roof welcomed her inside. Herbs and flowers hung from rafters, drying in various stages, the fragrance of jasmine, lilac, and mint filling the air. She pondered the mural she'd painted across all four walls of birds taking flight and those nestled in the tall meadow grasses—eluding to the winged elves who once could fly and now could not.

She started a fire at the hearth and peered into the ceramic bowl where she normally kept her sunflower seeds. Empty. One of her maids must have collected some to make a special treat for a friend—Calicia, most likely, and the friend, a handsome, unruly Mabara royal.

Serena would have to return to the meadow and gather some seeds while her water began to boil over the fire. Heading back across the meadow, she hadn't needed to return all the way to where Niall slept to find the sunflower seeds. But she couldn't help herself.

She hurried back to where he slept, and as she plucked sunflower seeds, she kept glancing at his sleeping form. Poor Niall.

He was good-natured, too, despite all that had happened to him where she was concerned. She sighed, stared at him for a moment more and then did what only the ancients were said to have done when they'd claimed someone who might be considered the enemy among her people. She plucked a handful of lilacs nearby, then kissed the petals and slipped them into the pouch at his waist.

If anyone should find him before she cured him of his sleeping sickness, he or she would have him searched, and they would know that Serena herself vouched for Niall. That he was under *her* protection.

Then with her basketful of sunflower seeds, she rushed back to the croft. She added several herbs, primrose, and rose petals, and five sunflower seeds. And would toss in the rest of the flowers and herbs as soon as the others had cooked long enough. Five minutes more to go.

But as soon as she heard men's hushed voices, she knew she was in trouble. Someone must have spied the smoke coming from the chimney of the croft. She was nearly done with the potion for Niall.

But all of her effort was doomed.

CHAPTER 6

Night cloaked Niall in a comforting darkness when he finally woke from his unnatural slumber. He blinked his eyes as he peered at the ebony sky sprinkled with shimmering, winking stars and a sliver of a pale moon suspended in the inky blackness.

A soft breeze rustled through the fragrant flowers surrounding his impromptu bed, the hollyhocks and sunflowers nodding sagely to him, but he didn't see any sign of Serena. Nor did he feel any better.

He narrowed his eyes. Had she left him here? Abandoned him? Intended to meet with her knight and tell him that Niall wouldn't joust him because he didn't have the strength? Or courage?

Annoyed to high heaven, Niall sat up. He had to have missed the joust.

He was about to call out her name when he heard male voices.

"They came here," Deveron groused.

By the gods, not Deveron. Niall lay back down and covered his aching temple with his hand and shook his head.

"I know, I know, my lord, but their fae dust is scattered so far and wide, I have no idea where they are. We've been searching for hours. They could be anywhere in the Mabara kingdom by now."

Niall didn't dare make them aware he was here. How could he explain why he had helped Serena to escape the Denkar prison?

Niall knew Deveron had never experienced such a horrible hangover as he still felt. But now he didn't want to explain further how he was to fight a dragon fae, and how he'd lost Serena in the bargain. Not only that, but he had no potion to counter the effect of the drug. Serena's abandoning him bothered him the most.

"At least she's back in her own kingdom and should be perfectly safe," Deveron said. "We'll return home, and I'll let Queen Irenis know." He sounded more relieved than angry.

"What about the count, my lord?" the tracker asked.

"He most likely has already returned home. Come on, let's go," Deveron said darkly.

Niall didn't hear anything more that was said between them and figured they had returned to the Denkar castle. He closed his eyes and groaned silently to himself.

When it was first light, he'd make his way to the

Mabara castle and let the queen know what he'd done for her daughter, how he had freed her from the Denkar dungeon, although he didn't want to explain that either, but he would. And maybe the queen herself would take pity on him and give him the antidote.

Then he was back to wanting to strangle Serena.

***

Oooh, Serena wanted to scream! She couldn't believe she'd nearly finished making the potion to give to poor Niall when her own trackers had the notion to look for her at her herb cottage in the wildflower meadows. And hauled her off to the tower. *The tower!*

Now she was confined until her mother reigned in her anger enough to speak with her. Serena was afraid to even mention Niall, and that he was dead to the world in the meadows, sleeping off the potion she had zapped him with. She had hoped she could get word to one of her lady companions to go to her herb cottage and finish the draught, then find Niall and serve it to him. Then he could go home. He'd missed the jousting tourney at least, and that was a good thing. She knew he could never face Sir Reginald the way Niall was feeling now.

She paced across the tower room, reserved especially for any of the royalty who dared disobey the queen. It wasn't used very often—mainly because her mother usually didn't learn about Serena's shenanigans—but the room was nicely furnished, thank the goddess.

Lilac cushioned chairs were seated near a high

window that let in light, when it wasn't night out. Softly padded, burgundy velvet benches were situated around the room for visitors who wished to visit with the incarcerated royal. Even a wardrobe sat against one wall for storing clothes, should the prisoner have to stay for more than a couple of days. Serena had left a couple of her favorite gowns in there for the occasional stay.

A curtained bed cloaked in burgundy took up one whole wall, the curtains and covers pulled aside just for her. A maid must have been alerted to take care of the task before Serena had been brought up to the tower. A warm fire also glowed at the stone hearth, and the chamber had been aired out.

So, the chamber wasn't that bad a place, certainly not like the Denkar dungeon Serena had been manacled in, except confinement *was* confinement. Understandably, the tower room was warded to prevent fae travel from it.

As the day waned and the night took hold, she realized no one was coming to speak with her. No ladies came to visit to let her know just what was being said among the courtiers, the guards ignored her entreaties to send a message to one of her lady companions, and the queen did not call on her either.

Serena could just imagine poor Niall waking and discovering she'd disappeared. She hadn't given him the antidote and had made him miss the tourney. She was certain he would be furious with her and no doubt believe she'd left him on purpose out of fae spitefulness or some such thing.

Sir Reginald, for all his blustering about besting Niall in the joust, wouldn't come near the Mabara castle. She had met him at the Renaissance fair during one of her forays to the human world in search of fun where she could still fit in while showing off her wings. She and the knight only met there because she was certain her people would never discover she was with him, since the dragon fae had claimed it as their own territory. Rarely did anyone cross them.

The first time she had arrived at Scarborough Fair in Texas, Reginald had immediately shown his interest in her, despite that she wasn't a dragon fae, and that she had wings. She loved being treated as someone special outside of her own kingdom.

Now she wondered if Niall, when he woke, would search for her. She hoped not, fearing it would go badly for him if he was found wandering around in the dark meadow or woods, searching for her. Then of course she would be questioned as to how he knew her and why he was looking for her. And who had drugged him and why.

She groaned and paced across the room some more, her stomach grumbling, and realized she hadn't eaten in ages. She called out to the guards. "I haven't eaten since yesterday at nooning meal. Will you have a platter brought up?"

Neither guard said a word. She really didn't think she could eat, not with worrying about Niall. What if her people found the dark fae wandering through the meadow and put him in the dungeon?

She couldn't ask about him. If they didn't know he was out there, they wouldn't send search parties. Hopefully, he'd return home to reveal to Queen Irenis what he had learned about the winged fae, although Serena was certain he wouldn't tell the queen about the kiss.

"Food?" she asked again, with a more appealing tone than a demanding one this time. She hoped she could scribble a message to one of the cooks who sneaked chocolate bars to her anytime she needed a fix. If she could only get word to Niall...

"Does the queen want her only daughter to starve to death?" she asked, her tone sharp, her patience gone when neither of the men responded.

She thought she heard the guards snicker. If she was queen, they'd be sitting in the dungeon. At once!

***

Deveron had the untenable task of explaining to his mother how they had not only lost the winged fae's trail at the Renaissance fair, but also lost track of her in her own kingdom. Niall had still been with the princess, and Deveron assumed that her mother, Queen Verbenia of the Mabara, would have incarcerated Niall by now. Although he also thought once Niall took Serena home, he would have returned to the Denkar. But when Deveron arrived at the castle, he quickly learned Niall *hadn't* returned home. No one had any messages concerning either Serena or Niall. Which worried

Deveron.

Maybe the Mabara didn't realize Serena had been in the dark fae dungeon. But how would the princess have explained having been with Niall? None of it made any sense.

Ritasia met Deveron in the hall leading to their mother's throne room before he reached the entrance, and she quickly pulled him aside. She looked fretful, and he felt her anxiety, too. As highly annoyed as he was with Niall for freeing the pixie-like fae, he was concerned about him.

"Is he safe? Have you found him?" Ritasia asked.

"Nay. Well, and aye. We found his trail in the meadows surrounded by a forest. According to our maps of the region, the Mabara's royal castle is a couple of days walk from that location. We don't know if they returned to the castle or not. But at least she's safely within her kingdom's boundaries."

Ritasia scoffed. "I don't care about the winged fae, dear brother. She has caused our poor cousin enough grief."

"Our cousin caused his own trouble. I still cannot believe he freed her from the cell!"

"Yes, well, you would have had to have done so as soon as our mother returned, and you learned Serena was the Mabara princess, not just any royal winged fae."

"True, but I would have brought her to see our mother and not taken her to a human Renaissance fair!"

"Why would she go there, I wonder?" Ritasia asked,

her head tilted to the side in puzzlement.

Deveron pondered her words. "Seems odd, doesn't it?"

"I'm going to check it out."

"I'll go with you."

Ritasia raised her brows. "I thought you were going to see Mother and apprise her of the latest news."

"It can wait. I'd like to know exactly why Serena took Niall to the fair first."

"Maybe you could get word to Alicia and the three of us could go?"

He smiled. Neither the king of the dragon fae nor the queen of the lion fae approved of Alicia and Deveron seeing one another until she was officially of age to marry. But that didn't stop them from making the effort every chance they could get.

***

Niall headed through the flower meadows for the woods in the dark, unable to sleep any longer, even though he still felt like he was trying to overcome some horrible sleeping sickness. Moving one foot before the other, he began to walk along a forest path. If there were thieves about, he dared any of them to mess with him as rotten as he was feeling.

He hadn't gone far while carrying a fae light to illuminate his way when he heard someone muttering away. He headed in the direction of the elderly woman's voice and soon spied a stone croft with a single candle glowing inside and a light that looked as though it emanated from a fireplace.

He knocked at the door, intending to get directions leading the quickest way to the castle. When the woman quit speaking, but didn't open the door, he hoped to set her mind at ease and called out, "I'm Niall and am seeking the Mabara royal castle."

The woman opened the door and peered out. She was gray–haired and hunched over, leaning on a hand–carved wooden cane, the top forming the head of a bird of prey.

"I didn't mean to disturb you," Niall said, politely.

"Why would you go to the castle? You are not Mabara royalty, are you?"

He shook his head, wondering why she would think that when he didn't have any wings.

"Come closer."

He moved closer and she pointed a crooked finger at his chest. "What are you?"

He pulled his golden medallion from his tunic. "From the Denkar fae."

"Royalty," she said, nodding sagely. "You are the one meant to marry the princess."

"My cousin is," he corrected, and for the first time since he'd learned of the news, he realized he didn't like the prospect. He tucked the medallion back inside his tunic.

She stared at him, then frowned. "But you have kissed her."

He had. But how had the old woman known? He

swiped at his mouth with the back of his hand, hoping that Serena's lip gloss wasn't shimmering on his lips again.

The old woman shook her head. "So you have come to ask the queen's permission to allow you to marry Serena instead of your cousin."

"No, Serena..." He hesitated. "We were in the meadow together, and she was going to give me the antidote for a sleeping potion, but she's gone and..."

"I see."

Did she?

Niall waited for the woman to say something more, but when she didn't, he said, "You wouldn't happen to know a cure, would you?"

The woman laughed, then shook her head. "But if she truly was going to help you, she will not now."

He couldn't hide his surprise, nor his concern. "Why not?"

"Her mother has imprisoned her in the tower until she weds Count Micala."

"Nay."

"Aye, my lord. If you want her help, you must rescue her from the tower."

Great. First, Serena shot him with this incapacitating potion. Then he had to rescue her from the Denkar dungeon due to her own folly because of painting on the wall in South Padre Island. And now he has to risk his neck even further to help her escape her mother's imprisonment in the Mabara tower?

"It is the only way," the woman said, with a definite sparkle in her soft gray eyes.

"You wouldn't know a secret passage into the castle, would you?" he asked.

"I imagine they would have them, but only the royal family would know of their existence." She glanced down at her pouch? "Do you have anything for me?"

At first, he didn't respond, not knowing what she meant. Maybe she expected him to bargain for information. He patted his pockets and found two gold coins and a little bit of lint.

"No, I have no need of gold," she said. She snatched the lint from his fingertips, balled it up and tossed it in the fire. The flames caught it and burned brighter. "What else?"

"I have a dagger I always keep with me."

"You will have need of it."

He dug around in his pockets some more and found...

Nothing.

Then he shoved his hand in his leather pouch where he kept human coins for when he visited their world. He juggled through coins and paper money, then felt something soft and velvety. Surprised, he pulled the items out to see what they were. A handful of lilacs from the meadow. When had they gotten there?

The old woman eyed the flowers with speculation, gazed up into his eyes, and he was sure she saw the puzzled look in them, then she smiled. She offered her hand palm up to take possession of the petals.

Once she had them in her hand, she peered at them closely, then took one and set it aside on her wooden table. The rest she tossed in a pot hanging over the fire. "I can use that in my tea. You will follow the path through the woods to the east. Once you reach the castle, you will go to the south side of the castle and climb the southeast tower wall. No guards can see that side. Use your dagger to grant foot and finger holds. Her room is near the top. You will see one window. But be careful. 'Tis a hundred-and-thirty foot drop to the paving stones below."

He wasn't worried. He'd just vanish and reappear on the stone below the tower if he began to fall. If he didn't fall asleep from exhaustion before he reached the safety of the ground first.

But he couldn't use fae travel to climb up a tower. Without ropes, how would he manage? Serena could probably get them to ground at that point if her potion did him in before he could get them to safety.

"Come," the old woman insisted. "Share a cup of tea with me before you go."

"But I must—"

"Humor an old woman. Come, tell me how you met the princess."

She reminded him of his grandmother, who was always trying to get him and others to stop and visit with her for a while. Seeing how this woman must be lonely, he felt badly that he had neglected his own grandmother.

He would visit her when all this was over.

"Are you all right out here by yourself?" Niall asked, as he joined the woman inside her croft.

"Aye. I am a witch, so the Mabara say. They leave me well enough alone. I am Magdana."

Not bothered by her revelation as he'd known several witches who were no more wicked than some fae, he nodded and glanced around at the croft. He expected it to be barren and cold, but a fire glowed warm in a stone hearth, and the walls were covered in pale blue, and murals of winged birds were painted over them, flying, or standing in the flower meadows, similar to the one he'd been sleeping in.

"You wonder about the murals," Magdana said, brewing the tea, then pouring it into two blue mugs. "Princess Serena is the artist."

From this to painting graffiti on the Denkar wall? Was there a message here, too?

***

A guard rudely awakened Serena in the middle of the night, and she knew this was not good. Her mother only summoned her to a meeting that late in the evening when she wanted Serena half-asleep and more easily manipulated. Serena rubbed the sleep from her eyes as she walked with her two-guard escort to the queen's chambers.

They'd even manacled her with anti–fae travel wrist links, which infuriated her. She wasn't going to slip away right now. Well, not until she had a talk with her mother. She would tell her just the way things were going down. She would marry the dragon fae knight, Sir Reginald, and the Mabara would have an alliance with the dragon fae instead of the lion fae. Both kingdoms were just as powerful, so what difference would it make?

Besides, her maids had said that the dark fae she was to marry was rumored to be dallying with some human at South Padre Island. Not that fae couldn't dally in a meaningless way. But if it got to be a regular thing with one human, that was a different story.

Her mother sat stony-faced on her throne in her sitting room and motioned for the guards to stand outside the room. She was wearing red, which always meant she was angry. Serena had heard other queens did the same. Must have been something they'd learned from one another. Want to go to war? Wear red.

Her mother's blond hair was pulled severely back like she did whenever she was unduly irritated. But when she wore her crown—the symbol of her position of power—that meant she would hear no objection from any of her courtiers, including Serena.

"Serena," her mother began, motioning for her to take a seat on a cushioned bench nearby.

Serena was afraid if she sat, she'd lose her nerve. So she stood and said, "I want to marry a dragon fae."

Her mother's eyes widened, then quickly narrowed. "Unless he is the king…"

"Oh, for heaven's sakes, the king is old enough to be my grandfather."

"Then you will not be marrying a dragon fae," her mother said sharply. Then she suddenly asked, "Where did you meet a dragon fae?"

Serena wasn't about to tell her the truth. If she did, she knew her mother would have men search the fair grounds and terminate any dragon fae who might be the one Serena was interested in marrying.

"You'll be marrying Count Micala and that's my final word."

"He's seeing a human on a frequent basis!"

Her mother dismissed her concern. "When he sees you, he will want nothing more to do with this human."

"And if he still does?"

Her mother shrugged. "Eliminate her." She smiled, her expression pure innocence, but Serena knew she was deadly serious.

"I want someone who wants me! And that I want back." She couldn't imagine terminating a human girl he had interest in, then expecting he'd finally fall in love with Serena instead. What kind of nutty thinking was that? "He hasn't even come to see me yet. To court me. To even pretend he's interested in this union."

"I don't believe Queen Irenis has reached him to give him word of the impending marriage."

"Oh terrif. Well, release me and *I'll* give him the word."

"No, you won't. It's his aunt's place to do so. And until that happens, you'll be locked in the tower for your own impertinence. I can just imagine you being a tyrant with the count and forcing him to want to end the contract. Beyond that, I will not have you seeing this...this dragon fae on the sly. If I learn who he is, you know what will happen to him. So be forewarned."

And *that* was the queen's final word. She called to her guards, and they promptly marched Serena right back to the tower.

Okay, climbing a hundred-and-thirty-foot tower in manacles without ropes couldn't be impossible if she could loosen the bars on the window, manage to slip through them, and find purchase along the brick wall, would it?

CHAPTER 7

Deveron, his betrothed, Alicia, and his sister, Ritasia, arrived at the Renaissance fair after it had closed for the night. A few security lights glowed high above, casting shadows over the treed paths and booths and stages where humans dressed in costume plied their trade during the day. Deveron lifted his nose to breathe in the hint of the aroma of turkey legs that had been grilled here earlier in the day, reminding him he hadn't eaten all day.

But what Deveron and Ritasia concentrated on most was the faery dust trails left behind in certain areas. The glimmering dust collected more where the fae had stayed longer—at a tavern that served ale. And at the jousting grounds inside the fencing, and in the building where the knights stayed before they entered the ring. Alicia still couldn't discern much about fae trails, having lived so long with the humans.

"One of the knights is a dragon fae," Ritasia warned,

although she quickly cast an apologetic look Alicia's way.

"Aye. And the others that frequented the tavern were also dragon fae. The fair seems to be one of their claimed territories," Deveron said.

They both looked at Alicia as if questioning her as to the identity of the fae.

She shrugged and folded her arms. "Don't look at me. I'm not a tracker, and I wouldn't know pixie dust from fae dust, let alone one fae trail from another."

Deveron cleared his throat. Pixie dust and fae dust didn't look anything the same.

"And certainly," Alicia said, noting Deveron's disapproval and giving him an annoyed look back, "I haven't any idea which trail belongs to which dragon fae."

"Hmm, so why would a princess of the Mabara come here?" Ritasia asked.

"To meet with a dragon fae on the sly?" Deveron ventured.

"Wouldn't her mother be upset with that? You said that your mother made arrangements with her mother to marry her off to Micala." Alicia made a face. "Even though my girlfriend, Cassie, still thinks he might come back and see her."

Cassie was human and Micala knew better than to have more than a passing acquaintance. Deveron frowned. "He was supposed to have wiped his visiting her from her thoughts."

Alicia scowled at Deveron. "Well...he...*didn't.*"

Ritasia waved her hand, dismissing the two of them. "If you're going to both argue again, I'll have to do this alone." She went back to tracing the knight's trail as she walked across a footbridge situated high above a creek, trees towering all around them.

"I told you that Micala better not hurt Cassie's feelings or he'd pay for it," Alicia said to Deveron as they followed Ritasia.

"I'll speak with him again," Deveron assured her. "I *did* command him to clear her memories of having anything to do with him, Alicia." He frowned as he thought about Micala's pretending to really enjoy Cassie's company. Had his cousin not been pretending after all?

He'd better not be thinking of stealing her from the human world. Not when he had a contract to marry the Mabara princess. Queen Irenis frowned on the fae bringing any humans into her kingdom for all the trouble they could cause.

"Where is he now?" Alicia asked, her tone sharp and accusing.

Deveron glanced at her, furrowing his brow in his best dark fae scowl. "How would I know? I'm *not* my cousin's keeper!"

"First, I had to keep *you* away from her! So that you wouldn't break her heart. Now I have to stop Micala!"

Deveron shook his head and started to walk after Ritasia again. "Sure, I targeted Cassie first because she was sunbathing on the beach and looked like easy game. You, on the other hand, were not even there as you were up the beach buying a couple of sodas."

Even now thinking back on that scenario when Alicia had thrown one of the ice-cold drinks at him, he'd barely reigned in his lion fae tendencies, then had darkly smiled, and vowed to get even, and still hadn't done so.

"But speaking with Micala isn't your job." He let out his breath on a dark sigh and turned to reassure her he'd take care of his cousin, but Alicia was gone. His mouth gaped as he stared at where she'd been, the leaves of the trees fluttering in the night breeze as if her sudden disappearance had ruffled them.

"I've got to leave, Ritasia. Go home. We'll come back tomorrow when the knight is here," he said hurriedly, ready to chase Alicia down, wherever she'd slipped off to this time. He preferred the time when she didn't have any way to fae travel, and he was in charge of where she went. She was too unpredictable now.

Ritasia glowered at him. "If I return home, you have to go. Mother will be waiting to hear what you have learned about the princess and Niall."

"I know naught, except that they had been in the Mabara realm."

"And here," Ritasia said, waving her hand at the jousting ground.

"Aye, and here at the fair, but I'm not telling Mother that. We need to learn what else is going on before we can give her an accurate report. You know how angry she gets when we give her reports that turn out to be false."

"Deveron, don't you dare leave me while you chase after Alicia! I'm not going home to face Mother alone."

Deveron gave her a wicked smile. "Believe me, it's no worse than my dealing with Alicia right now."

Then he disappeared, and Ritasia scowled. She knew just how they'd make up, and it wasn't anything like what Ritasia would have to face when she returned to the castle and the queen summoned her to learn what had happened to Deveron, the Mabara princess, and Niall.

Fine. If no one else was returning home, neither would she. Ritasia headed back to the shop where she saw the most comfortable looking hammocks hanging under a sheltered porch. If they truly were cozy enough, she'd sleep in one. Come morning, she'd be right where she needed to be to see who these dragon fae were and if any had designs on the Mabara princess.

And then she had a wickedly brilliant notion. If her cousin Micala was going to have to fight a dragon fae to ensure the princess's marriage to him came to pass in the event she was indeed seeing one of the Morcalon fae, what if...

Ritasia grinned. Yes, she had it. She knew just how to upset the proverbial apple cart.

***

At the stone croft in the flower meadow of Mabara at the edge of a fir forest, Niall finished the tea Magdana had made for him, but he wouldn't tell the old woman how he had met Serena. How could he? What if word got back to her mother? He was certain her mother would not like that Serena had painted the message on the South Padre Island building, nor that she had planned to avoid marrying Micala by marrying some dragon fae knight.

"You don't wish to say?" Magdana smiled at him. "You are kinder to her than she deserves, I suspect. Especially since she must have done this to you." She motioned to him. "I know she must have regretted doing so, or she wouldn't have offered an antidote. Which means you were not at fault for her carelessness."

"I startled her," he explained, not wanting Serena to be blamed for all of it.

"Ah, I see. So where has she been all this time? She had been missing far too long." When Niall wouldn't say, Magdana reached out her wrinkled hand and patted his hand as it rested on the table. "Has she been seeing you without her mother's permission?"

"Nay," Niall quickly said. "I had never met Serena before that…that day. And then I only knew she was of the royal Mabara house because of her wings, not who she truly was."

"Hmm." The woman leaned back in her chair. "You have met the one she is seeing behind her mother's back, eh?"

Again, he couldn't say. But he was surprised that her mother would know of her transgressions and had not stopped Serena.

As if Magdana knew just what he was thinking, she said, "Oh, her mother knows she slips off into the human world from time to time. It's our nature to do what we shouldn't. Ever since Serena was thirteen, she's been sneaking off to the human plane of existence to trick-or-treat during All Hallow's Eve. She's always needed confirmation that being different—having wings, whether in the human world or in our own—is all right. That she is accepted just as she is since there are so few of us in the fae world. But this," Magdana said, waving at the door, "this business she has of stealing away during the past few months…this is something altogether different."

Magdana sighed. "Her mother has been reluctant to put a leash on her, so to speak. Serena is much too free a spirit."

Niall admired Serena for it to a degree, but at the same time had reservations about her safety as she roamed about the world on her own.

"Do you know that she does not want to marry Micala?" Magdana asked.

"Aye," he admitted.

"But?"

Niall shifted in his chair. "We do what we must, as our rulers…" He hesitated, nearly saying "dictate," but then amended the word and said instead, "rule. For something of this gravity, we must abide our leaders' wishes."

Although if his aunt said he had to marry that

Venician Princess Lorelei who she had wanted Deveron to marry, he'd say no, and he knew he would have a fight on his hands. But the girl was sixteen and spoiled to the gills, and he didn't want to have anything to do with her.

Which again made him wonder if Queen Irenis *was* considering marrying him off also, like she had arranged with both Deveron and Micala without their input. Rumors were circulating that she was targeting Ritasia next, but who had Queen Irenis in mind for Niall?

"You shelter Serena from her mother when she needs protection from the one who leads her astray, no?" Magdana asked, breaking into his dark thoughts.

"I won't allow the knight to ruin her life," he said adamantly. He'd already made up his mind he would stop the dragon fae, knowing the knight only wanted Serena for the power it would afford him. Niall wouldn't let him get away with it.

He was certain Serena didn't feel anything but some misplaced admiration for the man. No great loss there.

"A knight? Really. How very interesting." The woman's eyes brightened with a calculating gleam. "Why would you do this? For the dark fae's honor? For your cousin's honor? Why not allow your cousin to do his own battle? He will win the prize after all."

Niall frowned at her. "That's exactly the problem. The knight sees her as a prize. A means to obtain power that he doesn't already have. A way to earn favor from his king within his own kingdom."

"Which kingdom, pray tell?"

Niall smiled at the woman's craftiness, but wouldn't say.

"You are most honorable, Count. You would fight this man so that your cousin could have Serena for his wife without lifting a finger on his own behalf."

"Nay."

"Nay?" She tilted her head to the side, looking mystified.

"What I mean is that I do this for Serena. Not my cousin. When she gets to know him, I'm sure they will be well-suited. But I won't allow the knight to ruin it for her."

"You do this for Serena," the old lady said, as if saying so reinforced the words.

"Aye. She deserves better."

"And you do it for your cousin," the woman insisted.

He didn't agree or disagree. He couldn't deny that he did indeed fight for the dark fae's honor and for his cousin's. But it was more than that. He didn't want to see Serena married to such a calculating fae.

"He's from one of the major kingdoms?"

"Aye," Niall said.

"But not your own."

He shook his head.

Magdana leaned back in her chair and looked solemnly at him, as if measuring him for the job. "So when you rescue her from the tower, then what? She will cure you and…?" She paused, but when he didn't respond, she added, "You cannot hide her from her mother."

"I have agreed to fight the knight. I must prove to Serena that he is not as honorable as he appears. I'm sure, as soon as we joust, she will see him as he truly is."

"Ahh. And then you will return her to her mother?"

Niall bowed his head.

"Where will the fight take place?"

"I cannot say."

Magdana considered him for a long time before she said, "I see."

"Her mother would undoubtedly not want her there," Niall explained. "So it must remain a secret. I must prove to Serena that the man is truly not suited to her, or she may very well always believe she has lost the one she truly loved, if her mother puts a stop to her marrying him."

"Hmm. I see. Will you wear Serena's favor?"

"The knight has already insisted she give it to *him*."

"Insisted? So he was afraid if he did not *insist*, she would give you hers instead." Magdana smiled as if this greatly pleased her. And then she said, "*You* will wear her favor."

Niall shook his head. "She wishes to wed the knight."

"Have you heard the story about the sun and the wind and their argument about who was stronger?"

"Aye. The wind blew at the man, who pulled his coat tighter to keep the chill out."

"And the sun bore down on the man with such

brilliance and bone-warming heat, the man soon removed his coat. The knight is like the blustering wind, trying to force the situation. You are like the sun, persuasive in a gentler manner. Free the princess from the tower and from the knight's clutches, and you will be rewarded as the honorable man that you are."

Niall did not think Queen Irenis nor Deveron believed he was an honorable man. Not after he stole the princess from their dungeon, then avoided them while they tried to track them down.

"I wish no reward other than ensuring the princess isn't matched with the knight."

"Good. Then you must away at once and rescue the princess. But you must also wear *my* favor at the joust, Count Niall." She opened a wardrobe, rummaged through it, then pulled out a shimmering gold veil. The fabric looked too rich and elegant to be the old woman's.

"Here, you must take this." She handed it to him with a faint smile on her lips.

He took the veil and tucked it into his leather pouch. As he would do with his grandmother when he took his leave, he grasped Magdana's hands and kissed her cheek in farewell.

He swore the woman's gray eyes misted when he hadn't meant to upset her, just show her the deepest respect.

"You will do," she said softly, "very nicely." And then her smile reappeared.

"We will bring Serena here once I have freed her

from the tower," Niall promised, feeling as though he owed Magdana for helping him, wanting to reassure her he had only Serena's best interests at heart.

"No, you must not say we have met. Wear my veil when you joust, but do not show it to her beforehand or she may warn you away from me. I'm a witch, you know."

He tried to hide a smile, not believing for one moment that she was anything but good of heart. "As you wish, Magdana."

Then he took off on the path through the meadow to the woods that she pointed out and hoped he would have the strength to rescue Serena without delay before he fell asleep again, or was incarcerated in the Mabara dungeon instead.

CHAPTER 8

Despite Alicia's grandfather, King Tibero, denying Deveron safe passage into the dragon fae kingdom, adamant that Deveron wait until she was eighteen before he could court her, he couldn't wait to see her. Deveron had to meet up with Alicia and ensure she understood it was his business to set his cousin Micala straight, concerning her human girlfriend Cassie. He knew Alicia's short temper could get her in trouble with the Denkar if he didn't stop her.

Black angry clouds hovered over the sky and even darker woods as he made his way to Crislis Castle where Tibero ruled. Winds whipped through the forest, scattering leaves, and Deveron felt as though a million eyes watched him from the woods. The dragon fae were known as the best archers of any of the kingdoms, and though some of them now knew who he was, several still didn't like it. Most wanted Alicia to wed with one of their own kind since she had so recently returned to the fold.

That's when Prince Grotto, Alicia's cousin once-removed, appeared out of the darkness, an arrow knocked as several other men appeared, bows in hand, but not moving to ready their weapons. Prince Grotto looked like he wouldn't hesitate to shoot Deveron if he didn't leave at once.

The sandy-haired fae stared Deveron down, his stormy green eyes challenging Deveron. "King Tibero said you would not see my cousin, until she was of marriageable age. What part of that ruling do you not understand, Prince Deveron?"

Deveron wanted to knock the dragon fae prince on his butt, sighing instead and decided this was not a fight he wanted to have. Only because he feared Alicia's grandfather would change his mind about allowing them to wed in the future. Not that Deveron would agree to it, but she was set to rule the kingdom after the king died. Deveron didn't want the haughty Prince Grotto to take over should Alicia be excommunicated from the kingdom for marrying the Denkar crown prince against her grandfather's wishes.

Not to say it didn't irk Deveron something fierce to have to put up with this pompous prince. Prince Deveron gave an exaggerated bow, then vanished.

Exasperated, he returned to the castle to speak with Micala about the impending marriage between him and Serena and to ensure Micala wiped Cassie's thoughts of anything to do with him. Micala and Serena certainly didn't need that potential problem between them.

Deveron quickly made his way to Micala's chambers. After knocking and not getting a response, Deveron opened the door and made his way to the curtained bed. Yanking the curtain aside, he found the bed unoccupied. Furious he couldn't resolve this matter at once, he began searching for Micala anywhere else that he could think of. After questioning the staff that were still awake and the guards on duty and learning that no one had seen Micala since early that morn, he began to get a bad feeling about this. Intending to speak with Ritasia about where their cousin could be, he knocked on her chamber door.

A maid answered, her eyes widening to see Deveron, quickly curtseyed, lowered her eyes and whispered, "She is not here, my lord."

Now Ritasia was also missing?

Not willing to deal with that yet, he stalked toward his mother's chambers, ready to tell her the bad news about Niall, although there was no way he was talking to her about Micala and Ritasia's wanderings, yet.

He wasn't sure what his mother might decree concerning Micala, but Ritasia? She'd be locked in her chamber under guard at once.

***

After stalking as fast as he could through the dark forest toward the keep where Serena was locked up, Niall finally saw the clearing around the massive stone castle jutting out on a high grassy cliff above the ocean.

Sea birds and the prevalent osprey that were hunting for fish soared high above, their calls carried on the salty breeze. Niall headed for the gates, surprised to see them still open at this late hour and even more astonished that he was allowed to enter the outer bailey without any soldier or guard stopping and questioning him.

Terra cotta stone walls stretched up maybe eighty feet while the towers at each corner of the wall walk were another forty, topped with gold cones that he imagined would nearly blind the viewer when the sun reflected off them on a clear day. The rustic castle keep itself, covered in green moss on the ocean side, sat squarely in the center of the inner bailey. It was surrounded by a second lower stone wall of fifty feet or so high. Beyond that, the higher outer walls featured two gates, the servant and merchant gate in the back and the front gates for more important personages to use.

Flickering torchlight illuminated some areas, leaving others in virtual darkness.

Guards walked the wall walk on top of the outer fortifications while Mabara, who were not royalty, put away their tools of the trade for the night.

Laughter peeled out in the nearby stables as Niall still expected someone to question what he was doing here. But no one did, which made him more ill-at-ease than if someone had asked who he was and what his business was.

The front of the keep loomed before him, but Magdana had said he needed to go south around the back of the castle where the guards would not see him. He thought that odd also as the guards who guarded from the wall walk would traverse the entire wall, which would mean they would come around the back side of the keep eventually.

Although he wished he could march straight inside, or at least try, and ask to see the queen concerning Serena's confinement, he could very well find himself in the Mabara dungeon. So instead, he took Magdana's advice and made his way around to the south side of the castle. Men and women were entering what looked to be the servant's entrance to the keep.

When the last person had left him in peace, he stepped back fifty paces and stared up at the tower where the princess must be imprisoned.

He remembered the faery tale of Rapunzel and how she let her hair down for the prince to climb up. The fae loved their faery tales. And he wished it could be so effortless.

No vines clung to the stone to make the climb easier, only tentative toe and finger holds on the moss-covered, rough-edged blocks. Despite having walked so many miles through the forest tonight and the dragging weight of tiredness he felt from the potion, he had every intention of attempting her rescue at once.

Since lilacs were steeped in Magdana's tea, which he understood could make a fae more tranquil, he thought she might have combined the flowers with something else that had made him feel much more invigorated.

He wanted to call out to Serena, to tell her he was coming for her, to see her lovely face, a smile, anything to encourage him that she was even still there. What if he made it to the window, and she wasn't even in the tower any longer? Maybe released already? Or moved to a new location?

He had to be certain one way or another. He began the arduous climb, one finger hold just so, the toe of his boots following in slow procession. The climb took an hour, maybe more to reach the halfway point when Niall felt so tired, he wanted to rip the bricks from the wall of the keep and curse the night.

"Keep going, don't stop," he muttered to himself. If he let go and reappeared on the ground below, he would have to sleep and then have to start from the bottom all over again. The notion was unthinkable. But, Serena's drug was working against him.

"Keep going, don't give up now," he chided himself again. He'd never been one to give up a challenge. This time, like any other, no matter how dragged out he felt, he wasn't letting go.

And yet his mind—the tired part—was fighting with his sense of never giving up. He told himself it shouldn't matter that she was locked away in the tower—that if it was anything like the Denkar tower for troublesome highborn prisoners, it would be comfortable, not at all like the Denkar dungeon.

He told himself that two months wasn't all that long

to have to suffer this sickness if he couldn't reach her before he was caught. Yet no matter how much he told himself it was no big deal, he couldn't bear the thought of seeing her in confinement again—the free spirit that she was.

"Toss down your golden hair, Princess," he wanted to shout because he was going to rescue her if it killed him.

But after another hour, of resting and climbing and resting again, he was still only three quarters of the way to the top, his strength dwindling to nearly nothing.

He whispered Serena's name as if calling to her reminded him how important his mission was. His fingers slipped, and he swallowed a curse.

Serena poked her head out of the window and said in a horrified, hushed voice, "Niall," right before he fell.

***

Her heart nearly leaping out of her chest, Serena squashed a scream as she watched in horror as Niall fell from the tower wall. One minute he was clinging fiercely to the rock wall, the next, he was plummeting. She could do nothing but keep an eye on him, her eyes filling with tears as she leaned as far out the window as the bars would permit, praying to every god and goddess that she knew that he'd make it safely to the ground using his fae travel ability before it was too late.

Furious with herself again for having dosed him with the sleeping potion, she saw him vanish, and she gave a deep sigh of relief. He had stopped his fall. But where had he gone?

Then she saw him standing shakily on the ground, staring up at her with half-lidded eyes. "Serena," he mouthed.

"Niall," she said back, blinking back hot tears.

Oh, how she wished she could take back what she'd done to him. She couldn't believe he was trying to reach her at his peril. Just to free her? Well, and to get the potion to offset how he was feeling. But still, she was certain that Sir Reginald would never have made half the effort to get her free for *any* reason.

She tried to squeeze through the narrow bars, but Niall shook his head and called out to her this time, "No, I'm coming for you."

She stared at him in awe. She'd never met anyone that determined.

But then he cast her a tired smile. "After I sleep for a while." To her astonishment, he reclined on the ground and fell fast asleep.

She quickly examined the wall walk, concerned that even his words might have caught someone's attention. Surely a guard would see him sleeping on the stone pavement. But none seemed to be patrolling the area or the wall walk on the south side of the tower. And no one had heard his calling to her, which should have alerted someone to at least investigate.

Which was more than unusual. The Mabara royal guards were never lax in their job.

She stood on the velvet cushioned bench underneath

the window, viewing Niall, watching for any sign he was waking, until the effort of forcing her eyes to remain open became impossible. Exhausted, she sank onto the soft bench, intending just to close her eyes for a few minutes, then continue her vigil, but she drifted off to the realm of dreams instead.

***

Soaring above the blue waters, Serena flew with Niall and white-feathered seagulls, enjoying the freedom of flying so high in the darkening sky. Pink ribbons streaked across the fluffy clouds in the distance as the sun began its slow descent into the choppy water.

She could fly like this forever, though it didn't occur to her how Niall could be up with her here like this. She had wings after all, when he did not.

He smiled at her, the look so loving she felt a flush of heat fill every pore. She smiled back at him, wishing the flight could last forever and never end.

But something pulled at her thoughts…a noise that had nothing to do with soaring above the Gulf. A grunt. A sound of something scratching against stone. And suddenly, she felt herself falling, falling, falling back to earth in a sudden rush.

Niall! Where was Niall?

Serena rolled and fell onto a stone floor and instantly awoke. She sat up, trying to figure out where she was and realized she was incarcerated in the tower.

Niall! She instantly recalled the precarious position he could be in. Her heartbeat quickening, she jumped up on the bench and peered out through the iron bars. He was making the climb again, determination in his every foot and hand placement and in the firm expression he wore. She examined him with fresh eyes. He was a wonder—a real hero, appearing unconcerned about whether he would get caught and be thrown into the Mabara dungeon or not. He had only one thought in mind: reach her place of imprisonment.

Then she narrowed her eyes. He hadn't bribed the guards to look the other way, had he? Not that she would fault him for it, and would in fact applaud his ingenuity, but the guards would have to be taken to task if it was so.

After another hour of watching Niall and wishing to the goddess that she could aid him in some way, he was getting so close, she thought he might make it. The black sky was already beginning to turn fireball red, warning the sun was on the rise. If he could free her from the tower soon, they could use fae travel to alight somewhere safe from here.

He was panting and dribbles of sweat beaded his forehead, but he didn't stop. When he finally grabbed hold of the iron bars that confined her, she thanked the goddess, wishing she could drag Niall inside, and gave another soft prayer of thanks.

"Serena," he said, hoarsely, winded, holding onto the bars for dear life.

She hurried to bring him some ale to drink and helped him to sip it while he held onto the bars.

He actually smiled at her, looking grateful and not

at all annoyed with what he'd had to go through to reach her. "I imagine not too many fae would risk rescuing you from the tower after your mother—I assume—locked you here."

Serena wiped his brow with her silk sleeve and shook her head. "None would. You either are very brave or—"

"Desperate," he admitted with a dark look.

"Aye," she agreed, feeling guilty about his condition all over again. "How will you get me beyond the bars?"

He slipped out his knife. "The bars and the mortar surrounding them are very old. Ancient, I imagine." With one arm slung around a bar and his feet propped on a narrow ledge, he dug at the mortar surrounding one of the blocks holding the rods in place.

His face red and his breathing labored, he looked ready to collapse at any moment. But he continued to persevere, although she offered to take a turn. "The blade is very sharp," he warned and wouldn't let her touch it.

She attempted not to show how annoyed she was with him that he would not allow her to help. She would not cut herself, and she didn't want to risk losing him again.

Periodically, he would pause, and he would jiggle the bar. Serena did also as he chipped away at the mortar. It was another full hour before she saw it give and her heart jumped a little skip and dance.

His face brightened, and he yanked hard. She shoved, too, and he nearly fell from his tentative perch.

She grabbed his sleeve, although he'd already seized the cemented bars and held tight.

Then he wrenched at the bar again, and pulled it free and tilted it off to the side. He frowned at the narrow opening. "Can you squeeze through?"

"Of course." No matter how difficult it would be, she would do it, not risking that he'd have to work on a second bar forever also.

Even at that, she had to work at it for several minutes, sure she was bruising herself as she attempted to make her way through the narrow opening as he held onto the two bars nearest her. But she was going to do this no matter what, not willing to force him to have to work on a second bar. He was too tired, and he'd never last.

She squeezed and wiggled and pulled and pushed, expelling her breath to try and make herself thinner. Glad she hadn't eaten earlier now, she finally managed to shove through the tight opening. With one hand on a bar, she threw herself at Niall with so much enthusiasm as she grabbed hold of him, she knocked him loose of the bars he was clinging to.

Just as the door to her chamber squeaked open.

"Princess!" her mother's advisor shouted from within the chamber, apparently seeing her leap from the window. Either her mother had decided Serena could attend the morning meal, or she was releasing her from confinement.

It was too late for either.

***

At the Renaissance fair, Ritasia woke as she heard the first of the human merchants begin to arrive at the fair an hour before it opened. Even though Deveron hadn't joined her, she was determined to learn why Serena came here. Was it to see a lover?

If so, maybe he would be intrigued with a lion fae princess instead of the Mabara one, and then Serena would be angry enough to leave him well enough alone and marry her intended, Micala.

Ritasia slipped off the blue hammock where she'd slept the night and sauntered on the woodland path, crossed the wooden footbridge over the creek, and headed for the knights' arena. Not that she expected the knights to arrive this early. Later, maybe, when their first joust would be held.

Or maybe they practiced out back for a while in the morning.

"Hey, you!" a man shouted from behind her, his voice directed at her. She ignored the man. He could be shouting to anyone. Even though no one was walking in her direction. Had someone suspected she had trespassed by sleeping here all night? That she did not have a ticket to allow her to enter the fair when it wasn't even open to the public yet?

She certainly didn't appreciate the tone of voice he used with her, if his comment was directed toward her.

The long skirts and a vest of velvet, a silken blouse with full sleeves, and knee-high suede boots she wore made her appear as though she fit in, so she could have been working at the fair, newly arrived.

But when a hand roughly grabbed her arm, detaining her, she gasped, and she was ready to whip around and take him to task.

What startled her even more was when he spoke, gruffly saying, "Don't ignore me, dark fae."

CHAPTER 9

Princess Ritasia whipped around to see who had so rudely accosted her at the fair, but worse than that, that he realized she was a dark fae.

"Dragon fae," she said under her breath, in a derogatory way as soon as she saw the bulky man dressed as a monk. He gave her an appreciative smile. A brown woolen cowl cloaked his face partially in shadows, but his blue eyes sparkled with intrigue. She arched a brow, turned to jerk her arm away, but the man held fast.

"If you don't let go of me this instant," she said, her voice low with threat, "I promise you'll regret it."

He smiled as if he knew something she didn't. She intended to fae transport him and deposit him in the Denkar dungeon, and then return to the fair. But the monk quickly slipped a steel bracelet on her wrist and manacled it to the other.

"No fae travel, princess," he said, with a smug smile affixed to his face, dark eyes gazing at her with contempt.

She scowled back at him, the beast, horrified and angry that he would hold her hostage in this way. So, he knew she was a lion fae, but did he realize she truly *was* the princess, or was he mocking her?

She tilted her chin up. "Since I'm the princess, it seems you would be careful how you handle me."

He motioned to people dressed in velvet and brocade gowns who were filling up the fairgrounds before it opened. "Dozens of princesses are here and about. King Henry and his wife are the only ones we need concern ourselves with," he said coolly.

She snorted. "Human play actors." But it appeared as if the pretend monk didn't realize that she truly was the Denkar princess. "What do you plan to do with me?"

"When Sir Reginald arrives, he will decide. This is the dragon fae's territory and here, he's in charge. You have no business being here. Perhaps a real stay in our dungeon will suit you."

At the dragon fae castle of Crislis? Surely not here at this place. They couldn't have a mock dungeon, could they?

"Is the knight the one who will joust?" she asked, wondering if he was the one Serena was interested in. It couldn't be *this* guy.

"Aye."

"I must see this great knight and his jousting

prowess."

"He loses."

She arched her brows in real surprise. "Really? A dragon fae who purposefully loses in front of a bunch of humans?"

"He prefers being the evil Black Knight."

"I see." Ritasia didn't really. Why would any fae lose the battle on purpose to entertain humans? The humans were meant to amuse the fae.

"When will he be here? I do not wish to be shackled to *you* for the rest of the day."

"In a couple of hours. He always has a late night of it. His reputation with the ladies must be maintained."

She shook her head. How was she to pretend interest in such a man?

The monk dragged her to a clothing shop full of ornately embroidered corsets and lace-up bustiers and skirts of velvet or cotton trimmed in gold. "You would look good in one of these sexy red bustiers," he said, motioning to her cleavage.

She gave him a quick tug and yanked him out of the shop.

"Here *you're* supposed to be a monk!" She pulled him so hard out of the place that she wasn't looking where she was going and ran smack dab into a knight dressed all in black—the silver fire–breathing dragon sparkling on his black tunic—the Black Knight, his blond hair in a braid down his back. A dragon fae.

She'd barely caught her breath, staring up into the

man's pale, narrowed eyes, his jaw twitching with tension before he spoke, "What do we have here, Tuttle?"

"She is trespassing. Do you want me to take her to our dungeon, Sir Reginald?"

"Why are you here?" the knight asked Ritasia, motioning for the monk to be silent.

Her heart thundering, she tried to come up with something that sounded plausible. "I have heard there is a knight so remarkable when he plies his skills in the joust, I had to see for myself if it is true."

"Did Serena tell you this?" the knight asked, his mouth curving up some.

Serena? So, *this* was the man she must have been seeing.

But then Sir Reginald sneered at her. "You are a dark fae. She would not have had anything to do with you or your kind."

If Serena had come here to see this man, Ritasia could not understand the draw. Yet she was determined to seek his interest so that Serena would see her folly and marry Ritasia's cousin Micala instead.

"Since you are dressed as the Black Knight, I assume you accept defeat in this human event. I admire your ability to entertain the humans in that way. It takes courage."

He looked her over and gave her an evil smile. "This woman is really a lovely creature, despite being a dark fae. If you want her, she is yours. Take her to the dungeon."

"You would not do this to me!" Ritasia shouted.

"Come, princess," the monk said, grinning like a fool.

"You are an idiot," she said to the monk, and motioned to the knight, including him also, "and you are as well."

At the blink of an eye, she was no longer at the fair, but in a dark, dank cell. Heart pounding, she was momentarily unable to think of what she could do next.

One small barred window let in a little fresh air, but she heard the squeaking of some rodents, rats or mice, scurrying about in the place, hopefully not in her cell. A single straw–filled mattress was lying on a metal rack in the chilly, unlit room, although the light filtered through the narrow window.

She was definitely not into self-sacrifice and was ready to tell all, *and then some,* who she was to spring herself from here.

"What have we here, Tuttle," a man asked, his tone brusque and dark, startling her.

Thinking she was alone, she felt her heart give a hard thump as she turned to see the burly man standing in the cell's doorway. He folded his arms, his whiskered face dirty, his blond hair in greasy straggles hanging over his shoulders. Tuttle, the monk, was standing beside him, looking perfectly pleased with himself to have brought a prisoner here, his smile odiously self-important.

The other man, probably the jailer, wore a gray tunic

covered in smudges of grime. A set of brass keys dangled off a chain belt at his bulging waistline. She longingly eyed the ring of keys, making him smile. Two front teeth were missing. Knocked out by a prisoner? Or bad hygiene? From the looks of it, he probably never brushed his teeth either. At least not the yellowed and brown ones that were left.

"She is a dark fae who was spying on us at the fair. I am certain the Denkar sent her there since that Count Micala is to wed Princess Serena, and his people are trying to learn what is going on with the princess," the monk said.

"You must report this to Prince Grotto."

"After I have my fun with her, Sir Reginald said," the monk pronounced, leering at Ritasia.

"A monk of some order," she repeated, trying to remind him of his pretend duty.

The guard shook his head. "Now."

"Why not report this to the princess?" Tuttle asked, sounding annoyed.

"She has slipped away again, and the king is furious. This one is of the Denkar, so the prince will have to question her since the princess is not here to do so."

"He will want her," Tuttle grumbled, then stalked out of the cell.

The guard immediately manacled Ritasia to the bed. As she lay down, she wondered whether this was the same cell where her brother had once been held.

"I happen to be Princess Ritasia, Queen Irenis's

daughter, in case you care."

The man shook his head. "Tell your story to Prince Grotto. Maybe you can convince him of your faery tale."

So much for her plans to intrigue the Black Knight and steal him away from Serena and show her what a blackguard he was, right before Ritasia dumped him.

***

Six hours later, after reclining on the odious moldy mattress in the Morcalon dungeon, Ritasia heard footfalls headed in her cell's direction. She sat up.

Prince Grotto arrived at her cell door, blond hair pulled back in a tail, his bright green eyes measuring her through the bars of the cell in a most inappropriate way.

The guard pulled the door open. The prince stalked into the cell, looking superior as he frowned down at her. "What were you doing at the fair?"

"You are Prince Grotto, are you not?" Knowing that he was just from his conceited bearing and richly appointed clothes and because he was supposed to have questioned her hours ago. "Whatever happened to manners in your kingdom? I'm Princess Ritasia, daughter of Queen Irenis and the late King Tolliver. Now that you've made me stay in this foul prison for half the day…"

He smiled evilly at her. "Princess Ritasia would never be caught dead at a dragon fae affair." Then his face darkened. "What were you doing there?"

As Prince Grotto glowered at her, she thought she heard rapid footsteps headed toward them. But they were soft, like a woman's rather than a man's. Or maybe a child's. But why would either a child or a woman be visiting the dungeon, unless the individual was bound to be another prisoner? Yet, Ritasia didn't hear a guard's heavy footfalls in conjunction with the lighter steps. So, whoever it was, he or she couldn't be a prisoner.

As soon as Ritasia saw Princess Alicia, her blond hair pulled into a ponytail, her green eyes focusing on the guard, not on her, Ritasia smiled. The girl was to marry her brother and knew just who Ritasia was, so she would quickly set the pompous Prince Grotto straight.

Alicia immediately addressed the guard, not even Prince Grotto, for whom she had low regard, partly because of his objecting that she was here and now stood first in line for the throne.

"Tuttle said you had a female prisoner here that I needed to speak with," Alicia said.

"You weren't available," Grotto argued, not allowing the guard to answer her first, the prince's voice heavy with rebuke. "You are never where you say you'll be, now that you are able to fae transport at will. The king ought to—"

Alicia didn't allow the prince to finish what he was about to say, but turned to see who the prisoner was instead. Her eyes grew huge and her mouth dropped open. "Ritasia," she said in a hush as if speaking her name out loud was forbidden.

Ritasia gave her a bright smile, raised her manacled wrists, and said, "Would this be a good time for you to teach me how to improve my archery skills?" She gave Grotto and the monk each a scathing look. "I know *just* the perfect targets."

***

Many dragon fae courtiers came out to watch Alicia as she instructed Ritasia in how to improve her skill with the bow at the archery range. The area was surrounded by trees, except for a narrow lane free of trees where wooden stakes had been placed at three different distances for the competing archers.

Ritasia had hoped for a private conversation with Alicia, though she wasn't sure how her future sister would view the situation. Alicia *was* a dragon fae after all.

The problem was Alicia had hinted that spies watched her every move and even attempted to hear what she said to her ladies-in-waiting in her own chambers. But worse, she didn't trust any of them either.

"The problem is," Alicia whispered to Ritasia as she showed her how to hold the bow properly, "everyone here believes they have my best interests at heart. So, it is not as if they are working for some tyrannical fae who is trying to keep me in check."

"You grandfather, the king?"

"Well, of course, yes, to an extent."

Ritasia quickly added, "And Prince Grotto and his men."

Alicia let out her breath, admitting, "Yes, them, too."

"Are you truly upset with Micala for continuing to see your human friend Cassie?"

"Yes. You know that nothing good will ever come of it." Ritasia sighed, knocked her arrow, and released it.

"Very good," Alicia commended. "Next time, aim a little higher and to the left more to compensate for the breeze."

Ritasia readied another arrow. "Deveron wants to speak to his cousin first and take care of the matter."

"I know. But it doesn't seem to be working."

Ritasia let her arrow go. *Thwack!*

"Much, much better," Alicia said, praising her.

Ritasia beamed. "Another." She readied an arrow again. "He planned to speak to him last night."

"Well, did he?" Alicia asked.

Ritasia lowered her bow and said quietly for her ears only, "I don't know."

Alicia frowned and folded her arms. "You two are like the best of friends, half of the time annoyed with each other, and half of the time inseparable. You almost always know what's going on with the other."

"I sort of got myself in a bind and was stuck in your dungeon."

Alicia studied her for a while, not saying a word, then she arched her brows. "Not last night. I was informed you were picked up at the Texas Renaissance fair this morning and brought straight here."

"I was at the fairgrounds all night." Ritasia aimed her arrow and released it. This time it struck the stake several yards past the second one.

"Why? You knew it was dragon fae territory, right? I've heard Sir Reginald believed you were spying on my people."

"Not on *your* people," Ritasia said indignantly. "Rather trying to learn what a Mabara winged fae was doing there instead."

Alicia didn't say anything for a moment, and Ritasia wondered if she thought she was lying. But then Alicia threw up her hands in exasperation. "What on earth is a Mabara winged fae?"

It was Ritasia's turn to stare at Alicia in disbelief. Then she reigned in her skepticism, realizing that Alicia hadn't lived with the fae all that long. "Sorry. I thought your Morcalon scholars would have taught you all about the different fae kingdoms by now."

"Are you tired yet?" Alicia asked. "Do you want to get something to eat?"

Ritasia hadn't eaten anything since yesterday afternoon, and it was nearly time for the evening meal. "I'm starving."

"Good." Alicia motioned for a servant to take the bow and arrows, then grabbed Ritasia's hand and stalked toward the garden path that led to the keep.

Courtiers followed them at a respectable distance, and Alicia kept her voice low. "I have learned about the major kingdoms, the rulers, the important history, and some of the languages. I feel that I'm so stuffed full of fae knowledge I will burst if they feed me any more details. I can't keep everything and everyone straight. So, what is the winged fae's story?"

"Princess Serena is daughter of the queen of the Mabara. The only daughter of Queen Verbenia. And Serena is betrothed to Micala."

"I knew the part about her betrothal. I just didn't know the Mabara were winged fae." Alicia made an annoyed face, her mouth and brows pinched. Then she gave a small smile. "That could be good—if Micala must wed the Mabara. Then maybe that will stop his interest in Cassie."

"The problem is that Serena is interested in marrying the dragon fae, Sir Reginald."

Alicia didn't say anything as she led Ritasia in through the servants' passageway to the kitchen. The rest of the courtiers paused at the doorway as if not sure if they could stoop so low as to walk down the servants' corridor.

"Well, that presents a problem," Alicia finally said. "As a dragon fae, I have to support my fellow fae, who seek alliances with another kingdom, right?"

Alicia was so new to all of this business, Ritasia had to smile at her. Then she sighed. "Yes, but you see it causes other problems. Micala is betrothed to her. Queen Irenis will not feel kindly about losing the princess to a knight of the dragon fae court, not when the queen had already drawn up an agreement with the Mabara. Serena's mother will be put on the spot also."

"And since I'm hoping to be Deveron's bride, if his

mother is angry enough with the Morcalon, she may say we cannot marry. Hmm. So what were you trying to do today at the Renaissance fair—*exactly*?"

Ritasia truly didn't wish to explain her failure but she did anyway, reminding herself that Alicia would be her sister once she married Deveron. "I was trying to encourage Sir Reginald to take an interest in me instead." Ritasia smiled when she saw the look of shock on Alicia's face. "Just for pretend. I have no interest in the knight. I must not have as much appeal as the winged fae."

Alicia shook her head and squeezed Ritasia's hand in a comforting way. "He was wary of your intentions, most likely realizing you had no desire to truly pay him any mind."

"True. Do you know what Tuttle said to me?"

"I'm afraid to ask."

"He said the knight always has a late night of it. His reputation with the ladies must be maintained."

Alicia cocked one brow heavenward. "Perhaps the knight doesn't have enough duties to perform. I will personally check into it."

Ritasia smiled.

They heard clanking of pots in the kitchen, cooks' voices, and smelled the aroma of freshly roasted game hens. Which reminded Ritasia just how hungry she was.

A guard rushed into the hall behind them, and Ritasia was sure he was coming to place her back in the dungeon. Although now that she was no longer shackled, she'd just fae transport out of here.

"Princess," he said quickly to Alicia, "Prince Deveron is at the castle gates, shouting that if Princess Ritasia isn't released at once, he will call in his army to storm the castle."

"My brother to the rescue," Ritasia said, seizing Alicia's hand and hurrying her into the kitchen. She was starving and wanted a bite of all that smelled so good in here. "Can you invite him to share a meal with us?" she asked Alicia, not about to give up a well-deserved meal for anything short of going to war.

CHAPTER 10

Niall caught his breath as Serena rested atop him in the faery meadow where she'd taken him when they'd fallen from the tower at her castle. "You could have warned me." She'd nearly given him a heart attack when she'd thrown herself at him and knocked him from the bars he'd been holding onto for dear life as tired as he'd been. Before he'd fallen to the ground, they had landed in the meadow, cushioned by a bed of fragrant flowers that he remembered so well the last time he was here.

She smiled down at him, so wickedly innocent, pinning him to the ground. "You rescued me." But he noticed then, her eyes shimmered with tears that she quickly blinked back.

He combed his fingers through her silky, golden hair, thinking how very lucky his cousin would be when he wed the girl.

"We must return to my hut in the meadow for the

potion I was preparing. I was almost finished with it when they caught me. But as soon as my mother's advisor warns everyone I've disappeared again, the alarm will sound, and they will search for me everywhere. Probably here first since this is where they found me the last time."

He was too tired to move. But more than anything, he just wanted to lie here with her, breathing in the fragrance of the flowers, feeling the warmth of the sunny breeze, feeling the warmth of her body pressed against his.

She sighed as if she was thinking the very same thing. Then she rested her head against his chest, and he continued to stroke her hair. "You are beautiful," he whispered.

But she was betrothed to his cousin, he reminded himself.

She finally placed her chin on his chest and looked him in the eye. "As much as I hate to leave this place, we must."

She reached for his hand, grasped hold, and before he could say a word, she transported him to her hut in the meadow, filled with drying herbs and flowers, he recognized seeing before. He stared at the mural on the wall. The same one he had admired before with the brilliant blue sky and the birds flying high above or half-hidden in the meadow flowers below.

Before he could ask her anything to clear up his confusion, she made him lie down on a mattress stuffed with feathers. As he sank into the comfortable bed, he tried his darnedest to stay awake—waiting for her to finish making the antidote as she moved to a collection of bowls and began to add flower petals to one of them. But he worried also that she'd be whisked away again and abandon him if he closed his eyes. Unable to prevent sleep from taking possession of his every thought, he finally closed his eyes in defeat.

Serena hastily mixed crushed herbs into a pot of boiling water and cooked it for a few minutes. Then she added it to the mixture that she had already made, worried someone would come here looking for her soon. Glancing over at his sleeping form, she hated to wake Niall as sound asleep as he was, but as soon as he drank the concoction, he would feel revitalized enough to stave off the need for sleep for hours, just like he normally would do.

She crossed the floor to the bed and touched his shoulder, then gently shook him. He didn't respond. She said, "Niall, the antidote is ready."

He didn't twitch.

She knew it wouldn't work, but she wanted to anyway and leaned over to give him a kiss. As soon as her lips touched his, his mouth curved up in a small smile. Before she could punch him for being awake and pretending he was not, he reached up and grabbed her shoulders, pulling her down to embrace her...and kiss her.

She melted against him, feeling a surge of

something deeper for him, a feeling of connectedness that she had never felt with anyone else. She enjoyed being with him, even if she was annoyed with him. And when she was in the tower, all she could think of was reuniting with him. Not just to keep him safe from her people, or cure him of his sleeping sickness, but just to be with him.

When he lightened his grip on her, he said, "Waking me in that manner is preferred to any other." A hint of a smile played in his eyes, but he seemed serious, too.

"You faked being asleep," she scolded, so unfamiliar with the feelings that were welling up inside her, she wasn't sure whether to attempt to ignore them or glory in them.

He smiled then. "No. I heard your voice from far away, but not what you said. And then I felt your mouth seeking a kiss from me, and that's when I fully awoke."

But she could tell he was still groggy, the way his eyes were half-lidded, his speech still tired.

"Drink the brew," she said, pulling away from him to get the mug of the antidote, wanting him to feel so much better. She helped him to sit up and offered him the fragrant potion.

"It is not poisoned, is it?" he asked, taking the mug in his hands.

She frowned at him, folding her arms. "Why would I poison you?"

"Not you, Serena. You could not finish the process yesterday. What if someone threw something else in the pot in the meantime?"

She leaned over and smelled the concoction. "No, it has the right scent. Hurry, Niall, and drink up before we're caught. You don't want to wait to overcome this condition you suffer from for another two months, do you?"

Niall wasn't about to wait a second longer to get rid of this perpetual tiredness. He gulped down the fragrant drink that tasted like peppermint and lavender combined, not sure he liked the unusual flavor.

"I wish to go to South Padre Island," Serena said, much to his surprise.

"Why there? Do you still think I cannot joust successfully against the dragon fae?" he asked, not liking that she might believe that about him, but realizing as soon as he said it, he shouldn't have assumed that's what she was thinking. He set the empty mug down on a small table next to the bed.

"No, of course not. The Renaissance fair is only open on the weekends. With all the time that it took for you to free me from the tower, and the time that you slept again, the fair is closed now. You've missed your chance to joust with him anyway."

Before Niall could say anything further, she grabbed his hand and whisked him away to the white sand beaches of South Padre Island. He knew just where they were as soon as they stood in the middle of the beach, invisible to humans, the warm wind caressing their skin, the sun still high in the Texas sky because of the summer night, the songs of seagulls floating on the breeze.

When he was sure about most things, Serena was a woman who unbalanced him. One minute, he was in charge, the next, she was. And he kind of liked the way she decided things for them sometimes, not all the time, but sometimes.

He took a deep breath of the salty air. Something about the island not only reinvigorated him like the potion had done, but it also made him feel relaxed, at ease, as though all the burdens he was feeling were lifted off his shoulders at once. He felt lighthearted and for the first time since he'd met the winged Mabara princess, he wanted to just have fun—*with her.*

Humans strolled along the sandy shore, while others frolicked in the surf, but most were done playing on the beach early this evening.

But then his wariness kicked in, not so much of her, but of his own people. "So why are we here? If any of the Denkar become aware you are here again, they may very well lock you right back up," he warned, worried that any Denkar might spot them, report back, and the royal guard dispatched at once.

"In your dungeon again?" she asked, eyes wide.

"Certainly not. At least I assume they wouldn't. That is if they know who you are now. So why are we here?" he asked again.

She shrugged, pulled off her sandals, and smiled as the sand sifted through her toes while she walked toward the blue water. Her fae silk skirts fluttered in the heavenly breeze, and she looked as though she felt right at home here, and beautiful, just like the first time he had seen her, but this time her golden hair floated around her shoulders.

"Do you come here often?" she asked, glancing over her shoulder at him.

"Sometimes," Niall said, dumping his boots next to her sandals.

She turned her gaze toward the water again, and he yanked off his leather pouch and tunic. Then he rolled up his breeches so that they rested in wrinkly cuffs at his knees.

Humans could not see their clothes lying on the beach as long as the fae didn't put them on and then make themselves visible. So, their gear would be safe from thieves, unless a fae decided to steal the items. Which was a lot less likely than humans purloining anything left on a beach unattended.

"To chase after the girls?" She lifted her brows in question, her gaze shifting from the Gulf to see Niall's response when he didn't answer, and her eyes widened to see his golden chest bared.

"No," he said, belatedly, amused that she seemed perturbed by the notion he might chase after other wenches. Was she jealous of his interest in other girls?

He was loath to admit he felt that way about Sir Reginald's interest in Serena. When Niall had no claim to her!

***

Niall was gorgeous, his legs just as tan as his chest, his golden hair dusting his shoulders. Serena's gaze shifted to his face. "No?" she asked, sounding as if she didn't believe him, which she hadn't meant to. "Just ogling the human girls then?"

He smiled.

Self-assured fae.

She snorted and headed for the water as Niall followed behind her.

"What is the fascination with human females anyway?" she persisted.

"None."

Now she *didn't* believe him! She glanced over her shoulder at him, her eyes rounded.

"None for me. I cannot speak for other fae."

She *still* didn't believe him. Why would a blue-blooded male fae not be intrigued by the human girls wearing string bikinis? "What do you do here then?"

"Swim."

"Swim?" She reached the water's edge as it swept over her toes and pulled back. "You swim."

Looking sufficiently serious, he nodded. "Don't you?"

She fluttered her wings in an annoyed manner. "If they get wet…"

"You cannot fly?" he asked, sounding more than surprised.

She frowned at him. "I cannot fly, period."

"Right. I didn't mean that. I mean, oh, I don't know

what I meant." He let out his breath in a huff, looking like he hated himself for having said something so idiotic that might have offended her. He probably had heard the Mabara were touchy about having lost the ability to fly, even though it had been centuries ago. "Do they get…waterlogged?" he tried again.

"I…I don't know. They get wet in the bathwater, but it's not the same as swimming in that." She motioned to the Gulf where seagulls sailed overhead and small white caps gathered at the top edge of the breakers.

"Do you want to try it out?" he asked, offering his hand.

She studied the water, wanting badly to swim, but afraid her wings might drag her down when they got too wet.

"Come," he coaxed, taking her hand and gave her a gentle, reassuring pull. "If you don't like it, we'll go back in."

Serena tucked her wings back as she carefully waded into the water, hand in hand with Niall. She loved the small intimacy he shared with her when they held hands. Though she recognized that since she was betrothed to another, she should not be so bold with Niall. But it felt right with him, and besides, he was only ensuring she didn't drown. That was all.

She stepped off the shallower sand bar and into deeper water up to her collarbone, her eyes rounding with fear. He immediately pulled her to the next sand bar, waiting for her to agree to go out farther or stay here. She loved how concerned he was about how she felt. If she'd been with one of her fussy old tutors, he would have tsked, folded his arms, and waited until she got up the nerve to conquer her own fears. He probably would have stood on the shore, staying dry while he motioned for her to get on with the task.

"How do you like it so far?" Niall asked.

She wasn't certain yet. She took a tentative step forward into the darker Gulf and sank into the warm salty water up to her shoulders. At once, she felt both panic and exhilaration.

He joined her, still standing much taller, and wrapped his arm around her waist, making her feel secure and protected.

She relaxed, jumping a little to crest a small wave, looked up at him studying her carefully, and beamed. "I…I love it."

That's when his anxious expression melted away, the furrow of his brows disappeared, and he smiled broadly. "I like coming here to get away, to swim, to walk on the beach, mostly without anyone seeing me."

"And to check out the girls," she said pointedly, knowing he couldn't come here and not take his fill of the bikini-clad girls. She almost wished she had one of those shimmering blue ones she'd seen in the shop where the clerk was trying to talk the customer into buying the hideous dress.

But because of her wings, Serena could never appear on the beach unless hidden from the humans' view. Not at least until she had control over making her wings invisible.

As if he knew what was bothering her, he said, "Your wings are beautiful."

She glanced up at him. He looked dreamy-eyed and sincere.

"I didn't think other kinds of fae thought anything of the sort. More that we are oddities in the fae world."

He smiled down at her. "You're beautiful, Serena. Don't ever let anyone else tell you differently." Then he stiffened a little. "You're not worried that Micala won't want to marry you because of your wings, do you?"

"Micala." She scowled and pulled away from Niall. She meant to stalk off to the shore, but she stepped into a trough and submerged completely under the water with a squeak.

Niall was there in a flash, pulling her from the water, holding her tight. She sputtered and coughed, trying to catch her breath.

Before she could scowl at how ridiculous she felt, Niall lifted her into his arms and kissed her cheek, and headed into shore.

Serena felt like the proverbial drowned rat, yet his touch was heating her inside out.

"I can walk," she insisted, sounding horribly irritated.

"We can have another swimming lesson later," Niall said cheerfully, ignoring her complaint.

He didn't think she was a complete idiot?

"How are your wings feeling?" he asked, sounding concerned.

She unfurled them behind her and flapped them. "Wet."

"But they're all right?"

She sighed. "Yes."

"Good. Next time, I'll show you how to float, dog paddle, and ride the swells."

"As opposed to drowning?"

He chuckled. "I didn't expect you to fall in a hole or I would have kept hold of your hand."

"Thanks for the rescue," she demurely said, realizing this was becoming a common occurrence between them. Would Sir Reginald have taken her for a swim? Would he teach her to dog paddle and float and ride the swells of the waves?

"You want to go parasailing?"

She stared at him, wanting to so badly, but how could they do such a thing? With her wings, and no bathing suits, and...well, how could they?

Seeing the hesitation in her expression, Niall must have figured if he pushed her, she would agree. He grabbed her hand and raced with her down the beach.

"You'll have a blast. Parascending is another thing I love to do when I come here."

"But..."

He smiled at her. "We catch a ride. We don't pay. Not when we own the island and everything here is for our recreational enjoyment."

"But…"

His smile broadened. "Just wait and see. The wind is perfect for parasailing. See that man's harness is getting hooked up to the parasail? He won't run after the boat, but instead will resist the pull to keep his line taut. Then one to three steps and he's airborne."

"But he has a helmet, and he's wearing shoes, a life vest even."

"He cannot fae transport like we can if he gets into trouble. Come on!"

One of the two flight crew members holding the parasail signaled the boat to hit it. The motor boat took off, but not before both Serena and Niall grabbed hold of the man and held tight. They weighed nothing when they clung to a human like this, but they would make him tingle with a strange numbness.

The man settled into the harness as if he was sitting, and Serena glanced over his back at Niall, who was watching her, not the spectacular view.

She grinned, having the time of her life. She was flying! With a Denkar fae, who had freed her from the tower. What would her mother think?

She glanced at the view of a bank of clouds highlighted in ribbons of pinks and purples with the setting sun, the darkening waters below, rippling with small crests of white bubbles, at Niall, the man who had given her the most fun experiences she'd had in a long time—swimming and now parasailing.

"We're about 225 feet up in the air. What do you

think, Serena?"

"I love it!" He had to know she did from the way she was beaming.

She felt she could do this all night when she realized the boat was headed in closer to shore, then the driver reduced the boat's throttle. The flyer and the fae began to gently drift down toward the dark waters. And when the boat stopped, the man unhooked from the harness as he floated in the water with the fae. The boat crew quickly picked him up, along with the parasail, and a couple of fae—without the crew or the man's knowledge.

A first for a boat ride, too, Serena thought, happily satisfied. With the breeze in their faces, Niall pulled a wet Serena into his arms, and she snuggled against him, loving everything about him.

She smiled up at him. "Ohmigoddess, that was the most fun I've ever had. No Mabara will ever believe I actually flew!"

The man who'd paid for the flight talked away to the crew members, saying he wanted to try a landing on the beach next time. But Serena had loved landing in the water, clinging to the man's life vest and Niall's hand and finding that wet wings and all, she could sort of swim, kicking at the water with her feet.

She couldn't wait to do it all over again another day.

But as soon as they reached the shore and Niall carried her out of the boat and onto the sandy beach, she caught sight of Micala, the dark fae count she was supposed to marry. He was walking along the beach in full human view, his hand wrapped around a human girl's. Serena instantly scrambled to get out of Niall's grasp.

"What's the matter?" he asked, nearly dropping her.

She pointed to Micala and the girl. "That's who I'm to marry!"

Niall stared at the two of them, then shook his head.

"Come on," Serena said, tugging him in Micala's direction.

"What are you planning?" He sounded reluctant to take part in this venture.

"I want to see who the human is."

"We cannot become visible. We're both wearing fae clothes, or at least you are. I'm half–dressed, and we're both soaking wet and looking a little bedraggled."

"So we follow them in our invisible forms."

"What are you planning to do?" Niall asked again.

"I want to meet my groom-to-be!" She smiled at Niall, whose golden skin suddenly looked pale in the fading sunlight.

Serena studied Micala, his blond hair long like Niall's. Were his eyes blue also?

He was the same height as both Niall and Deveron, same tall, slim build, wearing wet blue and white floral swim trunks, bare feet, no shirt. He must have been swimming with the human girl just before they had arrived, and his gait was easy and relaxed. The human girl had wet, dark brown curls that the breeze tossed around, and she wore a hot pink bikini, showing off a great figure. On top of that, she was walking way too close to Micala, when he was betrothed to Serena! Micala and the girl were *even* holding hands!

Serena wasn't often jealous, but she envied that the girl could show off a great bod because she didn't have any wings to hide. Which was part of what got Serena's own people into trouble centuries ago when they coveted looking like humans and lost their ability to fly. At least they were smart enough not to lose their power over the air elementals.

At that moment, she had the greatest urge to whip up a sand devil and give them both a blast of it.

CHAPTER 11

"What is her name?" Serena asked Niall as she quickened her pace in the sand, and they drew even closer to Micala and his human girlfriend.

"Serena…," Niall warned, casting her a glance that said *cool it*.

But she wasn't going to fight her territorial fae tendencies, even if she didn't want the guy. If her mother and Queen Irenis said it was a done deal and she couldn't get out of it, she had every right to protest Micala's actions. "You know her name, don't you?"

Niall sighed. "Cassie. She's a friend of Alicia, Prince Deveron's betrothed."

"Why ever would a fae have a human friend?"

"She lived among them."

"Humpf."

Niall definitely was trying to forestall Serena's meeting up with Micala as he kept holding her back as if he couldn't walk through the sand that quickly. Maybe hoping to change her mind before they reached Micala and the girl and Serena made a scene?

But Serena was betrothed to Micala and if she couldn't get out of this arrangement, she would be stuck with him. No way was she going to share him with some human girl.

She finally shook loose of Niall's restraining touch and quickly moved to intercept Micala.

As soon as she appeared in front of him, Micala yanked Cassie to a stop and stared wide–eyed at Serena, no recognition whatsoever that she should mean something to him though.

"What's wrong?" Cassie asked Micala, her voice concerned.

"What's wrong," Serena said, her voice highly ruffled, although only Micala and Niall could hear and see her, "is that lover boy…" She waved her hand at Micala, then planted both her hands on her hips in an infuriated fashion. "…is betrothed to me! And *I don't* share!"

Niall gave his cousin a half smile, almost apologetic as if Serena was some poor excuse for a bride!

"If Queen Irenis hasn't informed you yet, you're to marry Princess Serena of the Mabara kingdom," Niall said.

"A winged fae?" Micala responded indignantly, his brows pinched together in a dark scowl.

"Well," Serena said in a huff, "not that *I* want to

marry one of *your* kind either, dark fae."

Niall cleared his throat. "Maybe we could have this discussion in...*private*." He motioned to Cassie, who was staring wide-eyed at Micala.

"What did you say, Micala?" Cassie asked.

"Winged fae, is what he said, in a totally obnoxious way, I might add," Serena growled.

Red–faced, Micala, probably figuring the difficulty he was in with having to talk to invisible fae in front of a human girlfriend, said to Cassie, "I just remembered I have a very important meeting I have to attend. I'll escort you back to the swimming pool at your hotel and see you in about an hour for dinner?"

"No dinner, no escort. Didn't you hear what I said, Count?" Serena asked, hands on hips again, wings outstretched, flapping slightly, showing her irritation. The gold ring around her eyes was reflecting off Micala's dark brown eyes, not blue like Niall's, she noted. She imagined that it was only a matter of time before the gold ring appeared around his.

Giving her one last dark look, he spun around and hauled Cassie toward a hotel. "Sorry, Cassie. I don't know what made me forget that appointment. Well, I do. Whenever I'm with you, I forget everything."

She smiled adoringly up at him.

Serena stomped in the sand beside her. "Oh, *please*, spare me the human dramatics."

Niall walked beside Serena and cleared his throat.

She glared at him. "What?"

"Maybe we could go to an ice cream parlor and get some ice cream or something cold to drink while we wait for Micala to join us."

"With her wings on full display?" Micala said incredulously.

"What?" Cassie asked so sweetly, Serena wanted to puke.

Micala's face reddened again. "Sorry. Just thinking aloud."

Serena smiled, loving that he was making a fool of himself in front of the human.

"All right, Micala?" Niall asked.

He nodded and before Serena knew what Niall was about to do, he transported her inside an ice cream shop. If she hadn't been so angry, she would have loved the decorum. A mural of the sand and surf and puffs of white clouds drifting aimlessly across the sky over the bright blue sea covered the four walls. Wisps of white birds floated on the breeze and white sand crabs nearly blended in with the off-white sand. Palm trees were scattered about, framing the mural at the corners of the walls. The painting looked like something she might have created.

Small white wrought iron tables and chairs were situated about the place, the chair seats covered in blue and white striped fabric, encased by plastic to keep them dry in case of water–logged beach customers like Niall and Serena. The shop was devoid of customers, while a guy that worked behind the ice cream counter dressed in a blue and green floral shirt and blue jeans, stacked disposable bowls on a shelf.

The shop was cold, had to be because of the ice cream sitting in huge tubs behind a glass counter, and she shivered when she appeared visible, her clothes and hair still wet from the swim in the Gulf. The place smelled sweet, and she took in a deep breath and smiled when she spied the chocolate ice cream, sprinkles, and chunks of chocolate. Not that she was any less annoyed with Niall. She turned to glower at him.

Niall eyed the clerk, making sure he was still oblivious to their being in the shop, due to the fact they hadn't entered through the door, which would have initiated the ringing of a bell. He quickly made himself visible before Serena spoke to Niall as agitated as she looked and cause further trouble. His hair and pants were still damp, and the rest of his clothes were still lying on the beach, but this was a beach resort and thankfully the shop didn't require shoes and shirts for service.

Serena wet hair dripped over her shoulders, her clothes clinging to her curves, and he tried not to look too much. Although when she gave a little shiver, he wished he'd had a towel to give her.

She worried about him gawking at human girls in bikinis? By the gods, he couldn't quit looking at Serena. He couldn't even imagine how beautiful she'd be in a bikini with her wings displayed behind her.

"I didn't appreciate your interference," she snapped at him. "I had every right to speak my mind to Micala, my *betrothed*."

Niall smiled, which seemed to surprise her as her eyes widened a bit. Did she think he'd be upset with her for not treating his cousin better? He didn't blame her in the least and if the roles had been reversed, he probably would have tripped Cassie in the sand. Although he knew the girl and liked her well enough. He only would have considered tripping her if he had been Serena.

"What would you like to eat?" Niall asked Serena.

Her attention shifted to the canisters of ice cream. "Ice cream? Really?"

"Sure."

"Hot fudge sundae with nuts and whipped cream and a cherry on top. But chocolate ice cream. Not vanilla. And chocolate sprinkles."

He grinned at her and bought her a double dip of a hot fudge sundae, then bought another, but this one had mint chocolate chip ice cream instead.

"Hmm," she said, eyeing his sundae. "Is it as good as it looks?"

He offered her a spoonful. She slipped the spoon in her mouth and swirled the mint and chocolate in her mouth. "That's really good." Then she frowned at him again, and pointed her spoon at him before she scooped up a bite of her own sundae. "I'm not done being mad at you."

But as soon as Micala stalked into the shop, scowling, she looked like she was about to throw her ice cream at him.

Niall quickly offered her a seat, though she didn't sit.

"What is this all about?" Micala asked Niall, as if the winged fae didn't exist.

Which piqued her fury even further. Her cheeks flamed red and she glowered at him with gold rings ever widening around her eyes.

"Pay the man for our ice cream," Niall said. "We came here so quickly, my pouch of coins is on the beach still."

Micala cursed under his breath, giving Niall a dark look.

"I'll pay you back later."

"He's the one who forced us to come here," Serena said, taking another spoonful of her ice cream. "You shouldn't have to pay him back."

Micala eyed her for a moment, shook his head, then stalked over to the counter and handed the man the required payment. When he returned to the table, Niall said, "It's true. Our aunt signed the betrothal agreement."

Micala folded his arms. "I won't marry her."

"Why? Because you're stuck on a human?" Serena asked, the rim of her eyes glowing an even brighter gold—Niall had never seen anyone's glow *that* brightly—and her wings lightly fluttered, which more than intrigued him.

Micala glanced back at the store clerk, who was watching them curiously, but then he said to Serena, chiding her, "You're a little early for trick-or-treating, aren't you? And getting a little too old for it, too."

"You're never too old to have fun," Serena said. "Adults have Halloween parties all the time. Isn't that right?" she asked the clerk.

He grinned, looking at her wings spread wide, and nodded.

"They might have Halloween parties, but that's months away. Not now. Besides, what does *he* know? He's human," Micala muttered.

"Yeah, just like that girlfriend of yours. And you better ditch her or else."

"Or else, what?" Micala asked hotly.

She cast him her most threatening glower. "Ask Niall."

Micala glanced at his cousin.

Niall shook his head. "You don't want to know."

CHAPTER 12

Micala turned his full glower from Serena to Micala. "What did you bring her to South Padre for anyway? Did Queen Irenis send you?"

Niall didn't have a chance to answer. Serena slammed her unfinished cup of ice cream on the table. "You know what? I'm not marrying the likes of you. No matter what my mother and your aunt decreed. I'll take my chances with the dragon fae."

"A dragon fae?" Micala snarled, his eyes narrowing.

Before she could vanish, Niall seized her wrist and shoved his hot fudge sundae at Micala, who barely grabbed hold of it when Niall yanked Serena out of the shop.

"No fae transporting in front of humans, Serena," Niall scolded, heading back to the beach where they had left the rest of his clothes and her sandals.

"I don't come to the human world all that often," she

sniffled.

He noticed then she was fighting back tears. "You can't see Sir Reginald," he said angrily.

She didn't say anything, just went along with his marching her through the sand, her wings wilted, her shoulders stooped, her expression one of dejection.

But he was still frustrated with her over her continued proposal that she would marry the dragon fae knight.

"I mean it. He's not the one for you."

"Where will we go then?" she asked in a beseeching manner. "The fair won't open again until Saturday. We have a whole week before the tourney, and you can joust against the Black Knight then."

"Home. I must take you home. You'll tell your mother you will attend the joust and—"

"She will *not* allow it!"

"What do *you* suggest?"

As they walked along the beach, she smiled up at him with a gleam in her eye like a mischievous fae would. "The sleeping potion no longer affects you. If you return me, I'll likely be confined to the tower for safe keeping again. And you can rescue me at weeks-end."

He shook his head. "Next time they'd be on the lookout for my return and incarcerate me for sure."

"All right then. Where do we go that's neutral territory? Somewhere that no one will give us a second thought and leave us be?"

"No place is totally neutral. Even though the sphinx

fae are supposed to be. If it suits them to let your mother know where you are, they will."

"Well, where else then? Someplace in the human world?"

He frowned at that.

"We cannot go there because of my wings," she said sourly, flapping them lightly.

"No, it's not that. I cannot be with you for a whole week without you being chaperoned. It just isn't done."

"Surely, there is someplace we can go."

"Maybe," he said finally, reaching his clothes piled up on the beach, "we could stay with a distant cousin of mine."

"A dark fae."

"Aye," Niall said dryly, not liking Serena's tone of voice. "She happens to be an assassin, so you would have to mind your tongue around her."

To his surprise, Serena's expression brightened. "Does she use poisons in her line of business?"

Niall groaned. He could just see the two women getting along fine, and he would have to watch what *he* said instead.

He crouched to help Serena put on her sandals, and she smiled down at him. "Hurry, Niall. I want to meet this distant cousin of yours."

"I have to warn you Lady Sessily's father haunts Castle Armonjas."

"Really? How fascinating!"

"And she's taken an interest in a cobra fae."

Serena's eyes rounded.

"She might be entertaining him and not like the intrusion."

Serena smiled again and helped Niall with his tunic. "Nonsense. We can share secrets about our potions."

Her comment surprised him because no fae from another kingdom would do such a thing unless she planned to marry into the family. Serena had to be aware of such a thing.

"Let's go," Serena said, taking his hand and waiting for him to transport them.

"I don't want you to take up her occupation," Niall warned, not moving from the sandy beach. Then he spied Micala headed their way, his face grim.

Why was Niall ready to shove Serena behind his back in protective mode, when she was betrothed to Micala, not him?

"Where are you taking her?" Micala asked, sounding perturbed.

"What do you care, dark fae?" Serena asked, tightening her hold on Niall's hand.

Micala ignored her. "If I'm truly to be betrothed to the wench, I have to know," he said to Niall.

"We're going somewhere fun," Serena said. "You have your little human friend. Do run along." Then she looked up at Niall and smiled. "Hurry, Niall. I'm ready to go."

Micala reached out his hand to Serena as if to grab her wrist and stop her. "You aren't going anywhere until

I know your destination."

"As *if* it's any of your business since you have no interest in me," Serena snapped.

"It *is* my business if you're to be my bride."

"I'll keep her safe, Micala," Niall assured his cousin, but he knew if he told him where he was taking Serena, Micala would have the royal guard dispatched, and they'd return her to her own kingdom. Most likely she would be incarcerated once again in the tower.

He wouldn't permit it.

Micala opened his mouth to object, but Niall transported Serena first to the turtle fae kingdom where he briefly saw Lady Minxsta, their busybody distant cousin, in the kitchen herbal gardens. She waved to speak to Niall, her eyes bright as she saw him holding hands with the winged fae. The word would soon spread he had been spotted again with the pixie-like fae. First, word of the kiss went all over the place, now this.

Quickly, he transported Serena to a thickly forested area a few miles from Lady Sessily's castle in an attempt to allow Serena the opportunity to sufficiently sweep away their fae trail long before they reached his cousin's estate.

"Who was that dark-haired woman we saw on the grounds of the turtle fae castle? She looked dangerous."

"Aye, that she is," Niall agreed. "She will have word sent at once to the Denkar." He took a deep breath. "You will have to do your trail scattering while we make the long hike to Sessily's place. Can you manage the journey? Your sandals are not as sturdy as my boots for walking through this rough terrain."

She slipped her arm around his waist. "I will manage fine, as long as I don't have to return to the tower."

But it wasn't long before Niall was carrying her through the woods.

"I can walk," she insisted.

"You already twisted your right ankle. And next it will be your left. As dark as the night already is…" He didn't say anything more, figuring she got his point.

But then he heard horses walking through the woods. Instantly, he tensed and crouched down. It could be Lady Sessily or her staff, or any of the Denkar living in the sparsely settled area. Or it could be thieves, or worse, the same men who had tried to take Lady Sessily and the cobra fae, Prince Creshion, hostage on the outskirts of the cobra fae kingdom.

Duke Tully and his band of hostage takers were dragon fae, and they would not stop at taking highborns hostage, no matter which kingdom the royal fae resided in, despite that the Denkar royal guard had tried to take the men prisoner several times in the past. But if they learned one of their own knights intended to marry Serena, they'd whisk her away to the dragon fae's royal seat of power at Castle Crislis, Niall was fairly certain.

Serena patted her pockets and whispered in Niall's ear, "I have my weapons if they are our enemy."

"Your sleeping powder? And deadly poison?" he asked, surprised.

"Aye. I put them in my pockets when you were sleeping in my herbal cottage."

"Yours? Not the old lady's?" he asked, recalling that he had never asked about Magdana once he'd fallen asleep in the cottage.

"What?" Serena asked, her voice confused, her brow furrowed.

"I know I heard footfalls in that direction, just east of us, my lord," a man said.

Friend or foe? Without being able to see the men clearly, Niall didn't have a clue. And he and Serena were still about three miles south of Sessily's estate. But he wasn't going to chance having anyone take Serena hostage.

"We have to hazard fae transport," Niall said. "Even though it'll make it more difficult to eliminate our fae trail near the castle, I cannot risk having these men find us if they are trouble."

"All right."

"There they are!" a man shouted.

Horses galloped toward them in the thick underbrush, but the men reacted too late. Niall transported Serena to the front gate of Sessily's castle, torches lighting the entryway to the grounds where Welford, one of three guards Lady Sessily employed, appeared to be getting ready to lower the portcullis for the night.

He was wearing a navy blue uniform trimmed in gold that bespoke of the wealth Sessily had amassed while working as an assassin. Although the guards didn't often wear their best uniforms, except for show, normally. Since Niall was only Sessily's distant cousin, which meant just family, and she didn't even know he was coming, he wondered why the guard was dressed in his finery.

The guard shoved back his blond hair, frazzled by the wind, his sharp blue eyes taking in Serena, but only with a quick perusal, not a lengthy one that would have been insulting when she was obviously *with* Niall. Of course when considering a potential enemy, Welford would have studied her much more carefully.

Two other guards were watching them from the wall walk above, making certain that Welford wasn't about to have any trouble from the new visitors and most likely curious why Niall would be carrying a winged fae here in the first place.

She waved her hand behind Niall, doing her best to sweep away their fae dust trail with a high wind so that no one could follow.

The guard stared at her actions for a moment, his gaze on the wind that quickly left the area, then he smiled, and beckoned them to enter.

"My lord," he said, then glanced at the osprey fae again as Niall carried her into the inner bailey. Welford added with utmost reverence, "And, my lady." Not that he knew who the lady was, from the expression on Welford's face. It was more a look of surprise to see a winged fae in the dark fae's realm and perhaps awe because, if he knew anything about the Mabara, he would know she was of the royal household.

The winged fae were usually not known to mix with other fae kind much. Niall surmised that was the reason his aunt had wanted to draw up an agreement to have Micala married off to Serena—as a way to reach out to the kingdom, to forge a new alliance.

"I believe you might have trouble, Welford," Niall warned. "We ran into men on horseback in the forest a couple of miles from here. I didn't see more than two, but from all the noise the men made, I assumed others were with them. If they were Duke Tully and his band of merry hostage takers, you might want to lock the gate."

"Aye." Welford hurried to drop the portcullis, then closed the massive wooden gates. "Is the lady expecting you, Count Niall? She left no word with us."

"No. She was not. We hope that we may stay a while, if it is at all possible."

"Aye. The lady, is she injured?" the guard asked, motioning to Serena and the fact that Niall was carrying her carefully in his arms.

"Princess Serena did indeed twist her ankle."

"Princess." The man's eyes widened fractionally. "Lady Sessily will fix her up good in no time."

"She is a healer?" Serena asked eagerly.

"Oh, aye. I believe sometimes she wished she'd been a healer instead of a master assassin. But now, have you heard, my lord, that she has been accepted into the guild?"

"Aye," Niall said. "'Tis about time."

"'Tis said the cobra fae prince had something to do with it. Not that the lady didn't have the skills. She did. And she should have been qualified thrice over on her own. But that crusty old guild master would not permit a woman to hold the title."

"Aye, I agree. I often thought that Queen Irenis should have intervened, but her only advice to my cousin was to put the guild master out of his misery, permanently." Niall smiled at the notion and so did Welford. "I heard it rumored Lady Sessily had wished to retire from the business." Although Niall couldn't imagine being a master at her occupation and giving it all up as young as she was.

"Not any longer. She's on a mission and should be back anytime now, before supper, at the latest."

Niall wanted to know what had made her change her mind, but he wouldn't ask a servant in the lady's employ, although she had good relations with her people. They were more like family than hired hands.

Welford opened the door to the keep for them, and a woman, Sessily's loyal advisor, Venetia, hurried to greet them, her dark brown eyes widening to see the winged fae in Niall's arms. "My lord," she said, quickly curtseying, "and my lady."

"No word of the lady's presence here, or of mine, must get back to my family or hers," Niall warned. He knew that of any staff he had ever known, Sessily's was the most loyal. Loyal to her though, to no one else. He also knew that her people would do nothing, except make Serena and him comfortable until Sessily said what else she wished done. If she agreed to keep their secret, then Lady Sessily's staff would agree also.

Which was one of the reasons he thought of coming here. And, too, the castle was isolated from the rest of the Denkar, and because of that and her occupation, she didn't get very many visitors.

"I understand Prince Creshion has taken an interest in your lady," Niall said, as the woman directed him to a cushioned settee.

"Aye," Venetia said, smiling as she led them into the library. "He is good to us and good to our lady. I have never seen her so cheerful since her father died. Is your lady injured?"

"Sprained ankle," Niall offered.

"I'll get something for it right away. I'm Venetia, Lady Sessily's advisor," she said to Serena.

"Princess Serena of the Mabara," Niall belatedly said.

Venetia offered a quick curtsey again as if the other didn't count when she thought her a lesser royal subject. "Princess." Then she gave Niall a disgruntled look, most likely because he hadn't apprised her of just who Serena was in the beginning. Venetia smiled again at Serena and hurried out of the room.

"I'll be all right," Serena said to Niall. "It doesn't take that long for us to heal."

He knelt down at her feet and removed her sandal.

"Your ankle is swollen now, discoloring, and I know it has to hurt, especially when I see you wincing and—"

A man stalked in, white bearded, green eyes wary, interrupting Niall. He rose from his crouched position and bowed with reverence. "Lord Armonjas, may I present to you, Princess Serena of the Mabara."

"A winged fae?" The old man's eyebrows rose, and then he smiled wickedly. "Do you know the best poison to concoct?"

"Princess Serena," Niall said, ignoring the man's question, and she got the distinct impression he didn't want them discussing poisons and such right this instant, "this is Lord Armonjas, Lady Sessily's father."

Sessily stared at the wiry, elderly man, who didn't look like a ghost at all. Was this her stepfather and her real father dead?

CHAPTER 13

Lord Armonjas waved his hand at the introduction Niall had given to Serena and smiled brightly this time. "The potions, lass, do you know a really deadly one that works instantly and cannot be detected?"

A lady wearing black gowns, her dark brown hair coiled high on top of her head, a nearly sheer ebony veil covering it, swept into the room with a poultice in her hands and instantly addressed the old man, "Father, you no longer need to know of such things." Her dark brown eyes shifted to see Niall.

She smiled. They both greeted one another, and then she glanced at Serena, who wanted to leave the settee and not look like an invalid. Immediately, Niall rested his hand on her shoulder and made her stay put.

She would have been annoyed, except for knowing he didn't want her to injure herself further.

Venetia quickly followed behind her, bringing a

footstool and a couple of embroidered cushions to use to elevate her foot.

"It's so good to see you, Niall," Sessily said. She smiled at Serena. "And your friend?"

The way she said friend made Serena believe Sessily thought there was more going on than she was letting on.

"Princess Serena of the Mabara."

"Oh my. Of the osprey fae. How delightful. Rest up, and we will share a meal in a little while." Sessily turned her attention to Venetia. "Fetch them something to drink. I have to make a report, and I'll escort them to supper in a little while."

Serena didn't realize she'd even dozed off until Lady Sessily returned and said, "Come, would you care to join us for supper?"

Niall offered his hand to Serena, and she reluctantly stood, then looked down at her ankle and realized whatever poultice they'd applied against her twisted ankle had removed the swelling. The skin was still bruised, but even it didn't look half as bad. And walking didn't cause her but a twinge of discomfort.

"Your injury appears to be well on the mend," Sessily said, then ushered them toward narrow stairs that spiraled downward into a narrow corridor that opened up into a great hall. Servants were setting out the dinnerware at a long table.

"This is our cook, Mistress Teramond," Sessily said with obvious fondness, when the lady greeted them, her soft gray eyes shifting to take in Serena and her wings.

"Even Queen Irenis has on numerous occasions attempted to steal her away, offering much more money than I can afford to pay for her services so that Teramond will leave me and work for the queen."

Niall laughed. "She has a dozen cooks, and yet she could never have enough, I surmise."

Serena had expected Sessily to ask her why she was with Niall, why they were here, just something. Maybe she planned to over dinner, and the lady was still trying to decide how to ask the questions in a polite way.

That's when a man walked into the great hall, his blue eyes bright with interest, his dark brows arched in question. He bowed to both the ladies and smiled at Sessily in such a warm way, Serena was certain he loved her. He was tall like Niall, dressed fashionably like a royal fae would be, so she assumed this must be the cobra fae who was seeing Lady Sessily.

"Princess Serena, this is Prince Creshion of the cobra fae. And Creshion, this is Princess Serena of the Mabara."

"My pleasure," the prince said, his eyes straying from Sessily to Niall.

"My cousin, Count Niall of the major royal house of Denkar," Sessily said.

"Hmm," the prince said, bowing his head slightly in greeting. "You're a companion to Prince Deveron?"

"Aye."

The point was made. He was supposed to be with Deveron. Why was Niall with the Mabara princess instead?

Wait until they all heard, if they hadn't already, that she was betrothed to his cousin Micala!

Prince Creshion helped Sessily to sit at the table, leaning over to kiss her on the cheek while Serena couldn't help watching. He was extremely attentive to Sessily as if they were newly betrothed and he couldn't get enough of wanting to please her.

Serena humpfed at that, knowing how much her betrothed, Micala, despised *her*.

If any two people could be in love, Serena was certain the prince and the lady were. Why couldn't her mother understand that's what Serena wanted? Although when she thought about it further, Sir Reginald didn't treat her anything like Creshion did Sessily either.

Niall helped Serena into her seat, frowning as he saw the pained expression on her face.

"Your ankle still hurts, doesn't it?" The way he said the words, she knew he intended to carry her to her room at the conclusion of the meal.

And that's when she realized he acted just like Creshion behaved toward Sessily, only Serena was certain that Sessily had never knocked Creshion out with a sleeping potion first.

"Truly, my ankle is feeling so much better. Thank you, Niall." She wanted to say, *thank you with all of my heart*.

She noticed then others of Sessily's staff had joined them near the foot of the table and everyone watched

Niall and Serena's interactions, which brought a fresh flush of heat to every square inch of her body.

Niall bowed his head in acknowledgement of her dismissal that her ankle was troubling her, but the determined look on his face revealed what he was truly thinking. He would not allow her to walk again until he was certain she was perfectly healed. She couldn't help but love that aspect of him.

When he took his seat, she turned to Sessily, dying to ask about her potions and get the attention off Niall and herself, Serena queried, "Do you know the best forms of poison to make?"

Sessily glanced at Niall, and in that moment, something passed between them. Serena wasn't sure what.

Niall said to Sessily, "Serena makes poisonous potions and sleeping powder. The trade of the Mabara."

But still something was left unsaid.

Finally, Prince Creshion spoke up, "Are you marrying the young lady, Niall?"

Niall took a deep breath, eyed Serena, and shook his head. "She's betrothed to Micala."

"*I won't marry him*," Serena said vehemently. He'd flaunted his interest in that human girl even after she said he'd better not. What did she want with a fae who couldn't be faithful?

Sessily opened her mouth to speak, then smiled a little to herself and didn't say anything.

"So, the two of you plan to stay with Sessily for...?"

Creshion asked, fishing for a timeframe.

"A week, if we could," Serena quickly said. "I could teach you the best sleeping potions made by the Mabara, Sessily. Ask Niall. He has firsthand knowledge."

Both Sessily and Creshion glanced at Niall. He avoided looking at anyone while he buttered his bread, his cheeks tinged with color.

"Do you joust?" Serena asked Creshion, realizing belatedly she probably shouldn't have mentioned that, which was due to her nervousness in their company.

"Aye." A sparkle lighted Creshion's blue eyes. "Why do you ask?"

"Niall needs practice."

Again, everyone looked at him. And his face turned even redder.

"He needs practice at jousting?" Creshion asked, as if Niall wasn't in the room since Serena seemed to be running the show, and the prince seemed a little more than curious.

She wanted Niall to win the joust more than anything she'd ever wanted, which had her rethinking her interest in Reginald all over again. In fact, the only reason she even mentioned Reginald in front of Micala was to irritate him because of his fawning over Cassie. Certainly, she hadn't wanted to upset Niall.

"Yes, to fight a dragon fae knight. The knight practices constantly and would have an unfair advantage," Serena explained. "But we don't want anyone to get word of it."

Both Sessily and Creshion looked more than intrigued, maybe a little worried.

"Well, it's not something we want anyone to learn about," she said again, chastising herself for repeating her words—also indicating how unduly nervous she was.

They both nodded sagely, but they didn't seem very agreeable, their brows furrowing slightly. Everyone else at the table had stopped eating and conversing and listened to what Serena was saying.

Wringing her hands in her lap underneath the table and not wanting to speak in front of everyone, Serena felt she really had no choice and explained, "A dragon fae knight challenged Niall to joust because Niall kissed me." She meant to say that the joust was not over anything significant that could result in kingdoms getting involved. But she hadn't exactly meant to mention *the kiss*. Although that was certainly some of the reason for the ensuing challenge and she couldn't think of any other reason off the top of her muddled head to say otherwise. Not when every pair of eyes at the table was focused on her. Even Niall's. But his blue eyes had turned stormy.

She thought it was because she mentioned his kissing her, but changed her mind when he offered his own explanation.

"Which I only mentioned to the knight because I have every intention of stopping him from getting his greedy hands on you," Niall said, irritation evident in his voice and expression. "When you are betrothed to Micala."

Even though everyone tried to hide their gasps with napkins fluttering to their mouths or open mouths quickly clamping shut, she'd heard and seen enough to realize what a shock that was to the collected bodies at the table. She sighed.

So, she hadn't been thinking about the part about being betrothed to Micala either. In fact, she was thinking less and less of it where he was concerned, wishing now someone else might speak up and take his place. Someone who was frowning fiercely at her now.

"Right, but the challenge wasn't made until you said we kissed that he really got angry," Serena hotly reminded Niall.

Creshion looked like he was fighting a smile, his mouth quirking a little at one corner. Sessily still looked shocked, her brows marginally raised.

"But Micala is your betrothed?" Sessily said. "We don't get much royal news living this far out."

Serena had to acknowledge that Sessily was Micala's cousin, too, and the lady probably didn't approve of Niall's having kissed Serena for that reason.

"Micala didn't even know that we were betrothed," Serena said. "But he's got a girlfriend, *a human girlfriend*, and he can have *her* for all I care."

"Oh," Sessily said.

"Did you know about the girl?" Serena asked Sessily.

"No. We really don't get courtly news out here."

Serena ate some of her soup, part of a roll, and a few

bites of a game hen, then she asked, "Creshion, will you practice jousting with Niall?"

"When is the tourney?" Creshion asked.

"Saturday," both Serena and Niall said.

"Four days away. Yes, I'll practice with you," Creshion said, "but I'm a little rusty. Jousting isn't my main game."

"I have to admit jousting isn't my best game either."

Sessily stared at Niall in horror. "But you accepted his challenge! Why?"

Both of the men shook their heads at her. "A dark fae does not back down from a challenge from a dragon fae," Niall said.

"Here, here!" all those at the table said, including Prince Creshion, who was a cobra fae. But he looked like he was quickly becoming a member of the dark fae family, as well liked as he seemed to be among Lady Sessily's people.

"Sessily, I'll share some of my potions with you, if you'd like," Serena offered the lady, hoping to smooth things over with her, concerning her cousin, Micala.

Sessily smiled at Niall in a perfectly evil way. "What does Micala think of you jousting against the knight?"

"He doesn't know about it," Serena said. "Best if no one does."

"Only the dragon fae know of this?" Sessily asked, looking at once surprised and concerned again.

"Aye," Serena said.

"And if Niall should lose?" Creshion asked.

***

As she expected, Niall carried her to the guest chamber after the dinner had concluded, and she had been grateful the conversation at the table had turned to more mundane topics. Although she did object to his carrying her. Her ankle was improving all the time.

But Serena was sorry she'd brought up Niall's needing to practice before the joust. "I hadn't meant to mention about the reason for the joust. I really should have left it up to you to ask if Creshion would practice with you before this weekend."

Niall set her on a chair next to the curtained bed, folded his arms across his chest, and studied her for a moment before he responded. "Why did you?"

"I wanted you to do well at the joust." The reasoning for her asking Creshion to help Niall seemed clear to her.

An almost imperceptible upward curve of Niall's lips astonished her. But then his dark look was back, and she thought maybe she had mistaken that he was attempting to hide a smile.

"Have you changed your mind about the dragon fae?" he asked curiously.

She cleared her throat, hating to have to admit it, but not about to lie to Niall, knowing how much her saying she was going to marry the dragon fae bothered him. "I do not intend to marry the knight. Which is another reason I misspoke at the meal. You have no reason to train or fight the knight."

"Which is not going to happen, Serena. You know very well once a challenge is offered and accepted, there is no backing down from it."

"I don't want you hurt," Serena said simply, banishing the tears forming behind her eyes from making an appearance.

He drew close and knelt before her, taking her hand in his, his thumb gently caressing the top of her fingers. "If Micala should joust instead of me…"

"No!" she cried out, then quickly cleared her throat again. "I mean, it wouldn't work, would it?"

"He is a better jouster than me."

Her heart pounding with fervor, she didn't say anything. Deep down, she knew she should say, "*Yes, Micala should fight for the honor*." He was her betrothed after all. But even deeper down, she knew Niall had to do it. Had to as the challenge had been issued to him, not to Micala. But even more important than that, in her heart she knew he had to fight the knight because it was Niall, not Micala, who wanted her.

The tears sprang to her eyes this time, and she squeezed Niall's hand and bleakly said, "I don't want you hurt."

"Oh, Serena, that's all I have to know." And with that, he kissed her so passionately, she felt as though she had fae transported to the moon and back, her thoughts centered on his warm mouth on hers, then deepening the expressive kiss.

Several times she thought she heard someone

making small noises at the entry to the guest chambers, but it wasn't until Niall broke the kiss and cast a glance over his shoulder that she realized that they had been discovered.

Lady Sessily smiled a little tightly and said, "Come, Niall, we must talk. I haven't seen you in ages. And, Princess, do get your rest. The joust practice will begin right after morning meal."

Serena was pretty sure the discussion between Niall and Sessily was not going to be about the past, but about the present and future, and that whatever they discussed would all have to do with one winged fae.

***

After Serena went to bed, Sessily took Niall for a midnight walk in the gardens, and he was pretty sure he knew what she wished to discuss—Princess Serena and his involvement with her.

"What do you know about the princess?" she asked.

He glanced at Sessily, having expected her to ask something about the reason for the joust, but not thinking her questions would be concerning what he knew of Serena.

"She loves chocolate," he said, not feeling he owed his cousin any further explanation. "I took her to an ice cream shop."

Sessily slipped her arm through his as they strolled in the fragrant gardens. "How does she feel about the knight? Does she love him?"

Niall snorted. "No more than a rose loves a turnip."

Sessily laughed, then her expression turned serious. "You're sure?"

"Yes, of course."

"That's why you kissed her."

He almost didn't say it, but what the heck. "She kissed me first. It was a...payback, of sorts."

Sessily laughed again. "And you have feelings for her?"

"She's betrothed to Micala," Niall said dryly.

Sessily pulled him to a stop and gazed into his eyes. "You have feelings for the winged fae, Niall. Don't deny it. I saw the way you kissed her. You joust against the knight because of a sense of honor. But anyone can see the way you tended to Serena, you're much more intrigued with her than you'd like to let on. There's camaraderie between the two of you. Feelings. Caring. Your concern for her twisted ankle, getting her here to safety, even concern that she'd get enough to eat when the topic of discussion unsettled her. Your rescuing her from the Denkar dungeon at risking your own imprisonment, and the same with freeing her from her mother's tower."

"So, she'd give me the antidote for the sleeping potion," he explained.

"You brought her here, fearing for her safety with Duke Tully roaming the woods. Why not return her home? You don't want to give her up. And at dinner tonight, she said you took her swimming. And parasailing also?" Sessily arched her brows.

What could he say? It seemed a good idea at the time. The water had always drawn him in. And he thought she'd enjoy it also. He'd just believed that flying would appeal to her as well. As to all the rest, anyone in his boots would have done the same for Serena.

"The princess tells me Micala acts as though he despises that she is a winged fae."

"I wouldn't say he despises her kind in as much as I believe he was shocked that Queen Irenis would make the marriage arrangement for him without telling him. Then here he is with the human girl and Serena comes along, demanding he ditch the girl."

"I don't blame the princess. If I had been her, I would have felt similarly. So, had Micala come to grips with the marriage contract before you left him?"

"No."

"What about you? You do not seem to mind that she is a winged fae."

"She's beautiful. Inside and out. What can I say? I don't see her in any other way."

"But?"

"She is Micala's betrothed."

"That shouldn't stop you if you're interested in the lady. Maybe you ought to change Queen Irenis's mind. Seems to me you and Serena have a fondness for one another already and would make a better match. You are the same rank as our cousin Micala so that shouldn't be an issue. And as far as the dragon fae knight…"

"He's a non–issue," Niall said at once.

Sessily smiled and pulled Niall along the path again. "That means only you and Micala will have to fight over the girl."

That's what Niall feared. He had always been close to his cousin. He didn't want to ruin their friendship, but what if Micala realized his folly and learned all there was about Serena and he fell in love with her? And what if she returned the feelings if she was given half the chance to get to know Micala? Where would that leave Niall?

Wanting to joust his cousin next!

CHAPTER 14

First thing in the morning, Master Travis readied the horses for Niall and Creshion for the practice joust, while the guards cleared the outer bailey. Venetia had servants carry benches to the makeshift arena so that Serena and Sessily could view the proceedings under the shade of the armorer's workshop.

And Mistress Teramond served wine and cheese while other servants gathered to watch a spectacle none of them had witnessed before as Sessily had all given them leave of their duties during the practice.

Serena wasn't certain Niall wanted all the fanfare, and she worried, too, that if he did poorly, he might be embarrassed. But what if he did really well and Prince Creshion took offense? As good as he was with Sessily and her servants, a competition of skills could show a different side of a man. And he *was* a cobra fae.

Not that a dark fae couldn't be dangerous if he was

angry enough.

So, though Serena meant to sit and observe and attempt to enjoy the practice, she felt horribly tense, every fiber of her being taut with dreadful anticipation.

Sessily smiled at the two men and seemed at ease. But then she turned to Serena. "Does Micala know you are his betrothed?"

"Certainly," Serena scoffed. "Niall told him so on South Padre Island."

Creshion and Niall took their places at either end of the bailey, Creshion riding his own fine steed, and Niall on Sessily's borrowed horse, just as noble as Creshion's horse.

As the men rode forth, lances held, the men's anticipation of knocking opponents from their mounts, no doubt as high as Serena's, she held her breath. Wood smacked wood as the lances struck and cheers went up, but both men remained seated. Both paused at their respective end posts before riding forth and trying again.

"But Micala didn't give you any indication he wanted to marry you?" Sessily asked Serena as they watched the joust.

"Absolutely not." Serena had tried to control the way her wings would react when she was in an emotional state, sad, aggravated, happy—well, happy was okay. But she still hadn't managed to control that aspect of herself like she could school her facial expressions. Which meant her wings flapped slightly in annoyance, catching Sessily's attention.

"He was having too much fun with that human girl," Serena further explained.

"What did he say about you being with Niall? Was he jealous or anything?"

Serena watched the men tear across the bailey to prove their jousting skills again. "I don't think he was pleased." She thought about his demanding words that she tell him where she was going and smiled a little evilly. He wasn't interested in her, so what difference should it make if he didn't have a clue? He hadn't known where she was before that, so why afterward?

Niall and Creshion clashed again and both remained seated. Again, everyone cheered the two men on.

"They appear to be well-matched," Sessily remarked, a smile in her voice.

But would it be enough? Sir Reginald jousted constantly. If Creshion hadn't, just like Niall hadn't, then he might be at the same practice level as Niall.

"But you did tell Micala where you would be in case he wanted to check on you?" Sessily finally asked, returning to the previous topic.

"No."

Sessily turned her full attention on Serena. "Since he is your betrothed and not Niall…"

Serena waved away the notion. "Only momentarily. Micala is not interested in me. He's too much in love or infatuation or something with the human girl."

"Hmm," Sessily said.

"What?"

"If Queen Irenis learns of this, all of us will be in trouble."

Serena took her eyes off the men racing to unseat each other and saw the smile on Sessily's face. So, the lady wasn't concerned about the queen's wrath should she learn that Lady Sessily herself was harboring a wayward bride-to-be. Good. Serena didn't know where they could have stayed if not here.

Sessily shrugged. "Niall is a handful," she said, as if warning Serena not to get her hopes up about him.

Instantly wary, though not able to see that he would be, Serena asked, "How?"

Sessily smiled and leaned over to whisper in her ear.

***

The joust ended at a draw, neither man unseating the other. But they were of good spirits and both would practice that evening and again in the morning. For now, the servants hurried to do their chores. Sessily had a contract to fulfill and Creshion was worried about her safety enough that he went along with her.

Which left Serena and Niall alone to walk in the gardens covered in a light mist that afternoon.

"I am curious, Niall. Other than rescuing me from towers and dungeons, what do you normally do?"

"The most arduous of tasks, and I'm afraid I'm not very good at it."

"At what?"

"I am to keep Prince Deveron out of too much trouble. As his cousin, I serve as his friend, companion, and bodyguard. So, does Micala. But lately, the prince has had less time for us and spends more time with Alicia, which means—"

"I am the lucky one. What exactly did you intend to do with me when you found me painting on that wall?"

"My duty as a dark fae. Stop you, question you, and—"

"But you didn't plan to put me in the dungeon, did you?"

He shook his head. "I would never have put one as delightful as you in such a place." Though after she had knocked him out with the sleeping potion, he'd had second thoughts.

"Even if I had deserved it?"

He gave her a small smile.

She smiled back at him. "Will your queen be very angry with you for stealing me from the dungeon?"

"Most likely. But I wouldn't have done it any other way."

She nodded, satisfied. "What's your favorite color?"

"Pardon?"

"I know nothing about you. Your cousin said you were a handful. What did she mean by that?"

"Blue."

"What?"

"You asked my favorite color. I love the sparkling blue waters of the Gulf and the brilliant blue sky. It's cool and soothing and expansive."

"Ah."

"And yours?"

"Hot pink."

He raised his brows.

She smiled. "My mother wouldn't allow me to wear such a color. So, yes, I'd very much love to wear it. What did Sessily mean about you being a handful?"

"I dumped her out of a boat once."

"On purpose?" Serena asked.

"Is there any other way?" he asked, with a dark twinkle in his blue eyes. "You know what the dark fae's motto is? We don't get angry, we get even."

CHAPTER 15

All week long, Niall and Creshion practiced their heart out at jousting. And every evening after the last practice, Serena and Sessily, with her ghostly father making mental notes and suggesting them, shared poisons and sleeping draughts with each other. Serena was delighted to learn about love potions also.

By week's end, Serena had made a true friend in Sessily, and Creshion and Niall had become like brothers. Sessily's staff seemed to adore Serena and her winged uniqueness, and she delighted in the time she'd spent at the castle with Sessily and her people.

But the dreaded day of reckoning had arrived. Serena gave Sessily a heartfelt hug and said goodbye to Creshion and Sessily's staff, who had made her part of the family. But would Niall's practices have given him enough of an edge to work a miracle against the Black Knight?

Serena feared it would not.

***

When Serena and Niall arrived at the jousting arena at the fair in Texas, they expected the only spectators to be there that of the dragon fae, and maybe a few bolder humans. But the area around the jousting field began to fill up with the dark fae—the Denkar, having gotten word, stood beside the fence barrier to the west. A few of the turtle fae cousins of the Denkar were also in attendance.

Shocked and overwhelmed to see those present, Niall stared at the assembled courtiers that included Queen Irenis herself, her ladies-in-waiting, her advisor, Prince Deveron, Princess Ritasia, Lady Sessily, and Prince Creshion. Micala hurried to tell him he would serve as his squire, which pleased Niall to no end.

Most of all, Niall's grandmother, Anna, gave him a cheery smile and a thumbs up as Micala brought her a chair to sit on.

Who had told all of the kingdoms that Niall would be jousting against the dragon fae knight? His cousin Sessily had to have sent word.

The Denkar women dressed in garments of emerald green, sapphire blue, ruby red, and a smattering of gold satins and silk gowns, and the men in their tunics and breeches of the same vibrant colors filled the area in rampant support.

To the east of the jousting arena, the Mabara were gathered, wearing spring colors of peaches and soft yellows, robin egg blues, and mint greens. Their costumes were made in elegant silky fabrics, rippling in the gentle, hot breeze.

Queen Verbenia was flanked by both her daughter, Princess Serena, and Magdana, the witch. It didn't seem to Niall that the Mabara treated her with anything but respect. Instead, a man hurried to bring her a chair to sit in, and she was given the utmost reverence.

To the south, dragon fae filled the area, dressed in red and black satins and velvets. To the north where the human King Henry VIII and his queen would normally preside over the joust, King Tibero, his daughter, Princess Viviana, and his granddaughter, Princess Alicia, and a number of other notable courtiers filled the dais a story-and-a-half above the proceedings.

Minor scuffles ensued wherever humans attempted to slip in front of some of the fae to watch the unscheduled tourney. No doubt the unusual costuming of the courtiers, the fact no one wore human civilian clothing, and that the joust was not one of the typical performances, attracted human interest.

Even King Henry, the pompous human who thought to defy the proceedings before the joust began as only he would normally sit over the regularly scheduled events, while no others could be performed, was led away by an officious-looking dragon fae, who no doubt wiped the king's mind of what was going on. A female dragon fae shoved a mug of ale into his hand, and that was the end of the faux king's interference in fae affairs.

The event began with Niall riding a palomino into the arena. The Denkar, having learned somehow of the impending joust in ample time, had ensured the horse wore the symbol of the golden lion on his red cloth caparison, the fabric covering the horse's back.

And Niall was outfitted in the same colored tunic with the bold print of the lion over his chainmail, the gold veil that Magdana had given him to wear, proudly tucked in his belt for all to see.

Reginald wore a black tunic with a silver dragon shooting golden flames from his mouth. The knight rode a beautiful black horse as his mount pranced around the arena.

More minor squabbles broke out between dragon fae and the turtle and lion fae at the corners of the arena where west and south converged. The same happened on the southeast corner of the ring where the Mabara and the dragon fae had words.

Niall was surprised to see the Mabara royalty with their wings fully on display, not hidden as he would have expected when in the presence of humans.

A few fake human fairies had gravitated to the site, looking as though they wished to join the real winged fairies, but the Mabara would have nothing to do with them.

As soon as Niall and Reginald rode in front of their respective courts, cheers went up, but as they cantered past their enemies' temporary claimed spot of territory, jeers echoed across the field. Niall imagined the fae crowds and their enthusiasm for the sport as deafening as the fae's response put the humans to shame when the humans half-heartedly rallied for their pretend favorites.

Which of course brought even more curious humans to investigate what was going on that was eliciting such a large response in the jousting arena.

Finally ready and with only a motion of his gold and ruby ring-clad hand, King Tibero signaled for the joust to begin.

Kneeing their horses, Niall and Reginald galloped across the field, the heavier duty, six–pound lances readied, as weighty as Niall was accustomed to using. They rushed past one another, their horses' hooves sending the dirt flying and the hardwood struck hardwood making a resounding *smack*! The jarring motion traveled up Niall's arm with a jolt, but neither the count nor the knight knocked the other from his mount.

His heart thundering in his ears, Niall turned his horse and waited while Reginald reached the far end of the arena and readied himself for another pass. Serena was right, Niall had to admit. The Black Knight had the decided advantage with having jousted twice a day for the past several weeks. Niall had always been good at the task, but he could tell the way the muscle in his arm twitched from the impact that he hadn't shifted to balance in his saddle as well as he could, which meant he was still a bit out of practice.

Yet, Niall had the best motive in the world to unseat the knight and to bring honor to his people. With determination to prove the Denkar could trounce the dragon fae on their own stomping grounds for one of their kind attempting to break up a lion fae's marriage contract with the Mabara, Niall felt invincible.

But Reginald had a lot to lose if he should have to concede to Niall, while facing his king and his people, but with Serena and her kind there also, if he lost today, he'd lose much more than a lovely winged fae as his bride.

Reginald charged forth and this time he appeared to want to end this now, as if the first pass was only for show and now he meant business. Except Niall knew Reginald had hoped to easily unseat him from his horse the first time. What a boon that would have been. No contest at all.

With the sound of the horses' hooves pounding against the earth and the spectators perfectly quiet, the sun beating down on them mid-afternoon, and lances poised, Niall and Reginald clashed so hard, Niall was thrown from his mount.

Cursing to himself, Niall lay in the dirt on his back, not sure if he was the only one down or not. His people called to him, shouting encouragement, booing Sir Reginald as the knight's people laughed at Niall. He had the sinking feeling he had lost the joust.

But all he cared about was Serena and her welfare.

Micala, acting as Niall's squire, hurried to help him up, his cousin quickly saying, "Niall, you knocked the fire right out of the dragon. He's fuming mad, cursing out loud, not a good sport at all."

"He's down?" Niall managed to get out.

"Aye."

"I knocked him down?"

Micala grinned at him. "Aye. Though he got you, too. But you were well–matched. Despite that he's been practicing for weeks, and you're a bit rusty in the saddle. Just imagine if you had been training as long and hard as he has. He fell on his face in the dirt, not half as elegant as the way you landed on your backside."

Niall smiled, ready to do further battle. Although if Sir Reginald wished to end this as a draw as it was now, he would concede the joust was a tie. He didn't expect Sir Reginald to give up just yet, but it was an honorable way to end the joust. No matter what though, Niall wouldn't give up Serena to the dragon fae.

Once Niall was on his feet and had steadied himself, he bowed to his queen, which made the Denkar roar with good cheer as if they were one mighty lion. Then he turned to the Mabara, and again bowed, only this time he removed his helm and winked at Serena. Her pale face flushed crimson as her ladies giggled next to her. The Mabara went wild with cheers as the dragon fae attempted to outdo the Mabara and lion fae with jeers, boos, and hisses of their own.

With the help of his squire, Reginald finally made it to his feet, standing stony-faced, the once pristine silver dragon on his tunic covered in dirt, the dragon's flames doused. He didn't even acknowledge his own people, his rage building, his eyes smoldering with gold-ringed venom.

While Niall was receiving so much adoration, Reginald grabbed a sword from his squire and stormed across the arena toward him.

Micala hastily handed Niall an unfamiliar sword. "From Queen Verbenia herself. Her deceased husband's sword. The honor is all yours."

Niall glanced in the direction of Serena's mother, and the queen gave him a small smile and a nod of her head. Niall quickly showed his reverence to her, genuflecting, then rising to face the onslaught of the highly pissed-off dragon fae.

Their swords clanged and clashed as the two of them fought, the crowds now silent. Niall observed Reginald's swings, the way he was so full of rage and appeared to want to end this joust quickly with a kill that he wasn't fighting in the best form.

Twice, Niall swung his sword to his advantage as he kept his feet apart and his body balanced. Twice, Reginald fell back, only able to defend against the mighty blows.

But then Reginald roared and rallied his strength, swinging his sword as a man possessed. His sword connected with Niall's with a loud metal clang, tearing Niall's weapon from his hand.

A wave of worried "no's" and "ahhs" rent the air. Niall dove for his sword as fast as his heavy armor would permit. He heard running footfalls behind him, was pretty certain Reginald would strike him in the back to knock him down if he could. But Niall grabbed his sword off the ground, pivoted around, and connected with a swing of Reginald's sword.

The cheers were thunderous.

Despite having thwarted Reginald's dastardly move, Niall wasn't in the best of form when the brutal assault began. Attempting to widen his feet and crouch a little for better balance to resume the fight, Niall found himself defending and losing ground, rather than battling on the offensive.

He could deal with it though. He often practiced sword fighting against both Micala and Deveron. Both would gang up on him, forcing him to feel overwhelmed, beaten, unable to win. He always fought back as good-naturedly as before. Which was the only reason they had ganged up on him like that in training.

With that thought in mind, Niall smiled, recovered his balance and charged forth. One dragon fae was no match for him, not when he could hold his own against two lion fae.

Every blow he struck at Reginald was decisive and forced the knight to react rather than act. Niall caught Micala's look, saw the grin on his cousin's face as if he knew just what Niall had recalled about their own sword-fighting practices.

"Concede, Sir Reginald," Niall shouted, although the helm muffled his words and he was breathing so hard, he was sure his voice didn't have the command to it as he wished.

"Give up yourself, dark fae," Reginald said with a sneer.

They couldn't keep up this pace forever. Not in the hot Texas heat, not while wearing the heavy armor, although not as heavy as the human knights or fae wore in times gone by that could have been as much as sixty to ninety pounds. But it still weighed around forty pounds. And swinging the sword weighing another six or so pounds and crashing it against another with full force was just as wearying.

Reginald stumbled, and Niall paused, thinking he was ready to finally give in. The knight fell to one knee, and again Niall said, "Give up, Sir Knight. The battle is done."

Niall wanted to be standing at the end, not lying in the dirt in a worn-out heap, too tired to even summon the strength to fae travel away from here. He moved forward as the knight seemed unable to get to his feet without help and offered his hand. "'Tis done," Niall shouted.

But Reginald swung his sword and connected with Niall's leg, the sword slicing through the metal, cutting through his leggings, skin, and muscle.

Shocked gasps filled the air. Not even the dragon fae cheered their knight.

Niall fell to his knees, groaned in pain as the slice to skin and muscle burned with a vengeance. Blood soaked his leggings, and he tried to stand but couldn't.

Reginald rose unsteadily to his feet and lifted his

visor. "Concede the joust, yourself, dragon fae," he snarled and raised his sword as the winner.

King Tibero of the dragon fae stood and silenced the jeers of the Mabara and Denkar and the cheers of his own people. "We have one winner on the field today. Count Niall has that honor."

Micala tried to reach Niall to aid him, but Reginald pointed his sword toward him in a threatening manner.

Niall wasn't sure exactly what happened next. A sudden violent wind swept him and Reginald across the jousting field. Niall still had a titan grip on the sword Queen Verbenia had loaned him as he lay on his back near the dais where King Tibero had been sitting.

But Reginald had lost his sword and was eating dust when he tried to get to his hands and knees. Which, wearing armor, was impossible to do without a squire's help.

After that, everything grew dim. Niall thought Serena kissed him as Micala tried to stem the bleeding from the cut on his leg. He imagined he heard Magdana say Serena had herbs that would heal the wound quickly and something to make him sleep so he would feel no pain.

Deveron said, "I have never seen you fight so remarkably well, all due to my training strategy when I pitted myself and Micala against you. Are you not glad I did?"

Niall believed Queen Irenis said he could marry anyone he wished. And he was pretty sure Queen

Verbenia said she wanted the marriage contract rewritten.

But Serena's cool hands on his forehead and her warm mouth on his was the only thing that brought him to full consciousness as the dimness faded to light. Standing before him in his chambers while he lay in his bed, a dull ache in his leg and head, he stared up at the winged fae—an angel with wings of black edged window panes.

She took a deep breath, folded her arms, and frowned. "I'm afraid you lost."

"The joust?" Niall said, his voice a little rough. He shook his head. "You are *not* marrying that knight and no matter the outcome of the actual fight, I won."

"No, that is not what I mean. The marriage contract has been renegotiated. My mother insists I marry the fae who would dare attempt to rescue me from the tower after she put me there and after I dosed you with my sleeping potion."

"Only to get the cure," he said, brows raised.

She smiled, then frowned again. "And she further states she will only marry me to the fae who fought a dragon fae knight so valiantly to keep me from making the biggest mistake of my life."

"Aye, 'tis true it would have been your greatest folly."

She arched a brow.

He shrugged, fighting a smile.

"My grandmother said since you kissed me, it was a

done deal anyway."

"Your grandmother?"

"And because you wore my favor, even though I had not given it…"

"*Your* favor?"

"My gold scarf. The one Granny gave you. The one you wore tied to your belt."

"The witch?" he asked, confused.

Serena laughed. "She tells everyone who comes her way that she is a witch, but there's no truth to it."

"I didn't believe she was anything but kind and had your best interests at heart."

"Aye." Serena ran her finger over Niall's fingers. "She said she knew you were an honorable man when you vowed to protect me and wouldn't even reveal who I was seeing at the fair."

"I was afraid it would get back to your mother."

"So, you wanted to take care of the matter by yourself, without any backup."

He groaned. The first time he hadn't had any *backup*, Serena had put him to sleep.

"All right, but it means Micala is off the hook, and you have to accompany me trick-or-treating on All Hallow's Eve in the human's world."

He took her hand in his and kissed it. "You are too old for that."

"I will never be too old to have fun. And you have to agree to attend Renaissance fairs with me."

"It is Morcalon territory. I'm certain they won't like

it if we…"

She raised a hand to stop him. "Another fair. I have heard a great one exists in Maryland. We will go there."

"Which fae claims it as their territory?"

She shrugged.

He suspected she knew but didn't want to say. Which meant they were bound to run into trouble.

"And as soon as I ditch my wings, I'm going to wear a hot pink bikini on trips to South Padre Island."

"Only if you go with me, and only if you are invisible to the human population. Which means you must have your wings on full display."

She smiled brightly and sat on the bed next to him. "You really don't mind them?"

He reached out to touch one, his fingers like a brush of an eyelash, tickling her. "They're not fragile."

"They're beautiful," he said with real meaning, his gaze shifting to her face. "Just as you are. But no more painting graffiti on walls."

"I think we will have to return to the Texas fair and leave a message for Reginald once you are well. What do you think?"

He groaned, knowing if he said no, she'd most likely go by herself, and that he would not let her do.

***

A week later, after Niall was well healed, he and Serena returned to the Renaissance fair in Texas well before it opened that morning. He had attempted to keep her from returning, to no avail. In the end, he knew he could never lock her up to keep her safe, free spirit that she was. So, the next best thing was to attempt to keep her out of trouble.

With a smile and wearing a hot pink bikini and pink silky skirt to match, Serena showed him the brushstrokes to paint the Denkar message on the dragon fae wall, written in the dragon fae's language so the Black Knight would get the point. Except Niall couldn't keep his eyes off the bewitching artist, not caring a thing about the artwork. And he definitely wanted to get her away from here before any of the fae saw her as sexy as she looked.

Then for an hour, they curled up on the hammocks where the jesters had once reclined when Niall so wanted to after having been drugged with the sleeping potion.

When the fairgrounds opened, Niall took Serena into the woods and waited, hidden from fae view, invisible to humans, of course, watching the dragon fae gather at the tavern that served ale as they stared at the message. Some scratched their heads. Others shook theirs. One shrugged and threw his hands in the air in a sign of confusion. Even Sir Reginald was there looking just as puzzled.

"I don't think you wrote the message correctly," Niall said, smiling at her as he wrapped his arm around her waist.

She sighed, reading the message over again. "I wonder what I did wrong *this* time."

"There!" a dragon fae shouted, dressed as a monk in a brown woolen garment, his hood back, a rope tied around his waist like a belt.

All the dragon fae who were studying the message turned, their eyes widening to see Niall and Serena watching them from the woods.

"Get them!" Sir Reginald commanded.

"If you cannot read your own language, the message states: the good knight of the dark fae always wins!" Niall shouted.

Serena said, "That's not what the…"

But Niall had already scooped her up in his arms, embracing her tightly, kissing her soundly, and transported her to the Denkar-claimed territory of South Padre Island.

They were still kissing on the beach when the sun began to set, and at that point, Serena didn't care what the message said. The only one she cared about was the one Niall shared with her. With all his heart, he loved her, and she him.

Her wings flapped in an excited symphony, showing him just how much he meant to her.

But she still was puzzled about one thing.

"I still can't believe that Micala socked you in the eye before conceding that you and I were meant to be together."

Niall sighed. "It was the honorable way to resolve the situation since I'd kissed his betrothed. We had to resolve it that way, wherein he gave me a black eye, or fight me in a joust. And you know how that would have turned out."

"He wouldn't have won."

"He's a better jouster, believe me, Serena." He carried her to the water's edge.

"He *wouldn't* have won."

Niall looked down at her as though he was finally getting her meaning. "You...would have interfered?"

She smiled in her most sugar-coated, evil fae way.

"With your ability at harnessing the air currents? Sleeping powder?" Niall sighed. "'Tis good he just gave me a black eye, and you didn't unleash one of your talents on him."

"Aye. Now we can be friends...of a sort. Kiss me again, hero of my dreams. Send me to the moon."

And Niall did with heartfelt enthusiasm as she responded in kind, grateful their queens both saw the light before it was too late.

ABOUT THE AUTHOR

Bestselling and award-winning author **Terry Spear** has written over sixty paranormal romance novels and seven medieval Highland historical romances. Her first werewolf romance, *Heart of the Wolf,* was named a 2008 *Publishers Weekly*'s Best Book of the Year, and her subsequent titles have garnered high praise and hit the *USA Today* bestseller list. A retired officer of the U.S. Army Reserves, Terry lives in Spring, Texas, where she is working on her next werewolf romance, continuing her new series about shapeshifting jaguars, cougars and polar bears, writing Highland medieval romance, and having fun with her young adult novels. When she's not writing, she's photographing everything that catches her eye, making teddy bears, and playing with her Havanese puppies and grand-baby. For more information, please visit www.terryspear.com, or follow her on Twitter, @TerrySpear. She is also on Facebook at http://www.facebook.com/terry.spear. And on her blog at: https://terryspear.wordpress.com/

Follow her for new releases and book deals: www.bookbub.com/authors/terry-spear

ALSO BY TERRY SPEAR

Young Adult Titles:

The World of Fae:
The Dark Fae
The Deadly Fae
The Winged Fae
The Ancient Fae
Dragon Fae
Hawk Fae
Phantom Fae
Golden Fae
Falcon Fae
Woodland Fae (TBA)

The World of Elf:
The Shadow Elf
The Darkland Elf (TBA)

Blood Moon Series:
Kiss of the Vampire
Blood of the Vampire (TBA)
Night of the Vampire (TBA)

Demon Guardian Series:
The Trouble with Demons
Demon Trouble, Too

Demon Hunter

Non-Series for Now:
Ghostly Liaisons
The Beast Within
Courtly Masquerade
Deidre's Secret

The Magic of Inherian:
The Scepter of Salvation
The Mage of Monrovia
Emerald Isle of Mists (TBA)

Adult Titles:

Romantic Suspense: Deadly Fortunes, In the Dead of the Night, Relative Danger, Bound by Danger
   The Highlanders Series: His Wild Highland Lass, Vexing the Highlander, Winning the Highlander's Heart, The Accidental Highland Hero, Highland Rake, Taming the Wild Highlander, The Highlander, Her Highland Hero, The Viking's Highland Lass, My Highlander
   Other historical romances: Lady Caroline & the Egotistical Earl, A Ghost of a Chance at Love
   Heart of the Wolf Series: Heart of the Wolf, Destiny of the Wolf, To Tempt the Wolf, Legend of the White Wolf, Seduced by the Wolf, Wolf Fever, Heart of the Highland Wolf, Dreaming of the Wolf, A SEAL in Wolf's Clothing, A Howl for a Highlander, A Highland Werewolf Wedding, A SEAL Wolf Christmas, Silence of the Wolf, Hero of a Highland Wolf, A Highland Wolf Christmas, A SEAL Wolf Hunting; A Silver Wolf

Christmas, A SEAL Wolf in Too Deep, Alpha Wolf Need Not Apply, A Billionaire in Wolf's Clothing

White Wolf: Legend of the White Wolf, Dreaming of a White Wolf Christmas, Flight of the White Wolf

SEAL Wolves: To Tempt the Wolf, A SEAL in Wolf's Clothing, A SEAL Wolf Christmas; SEAL Wolf Hunting, SEAL Wolf in Too Deep

Silver Bros Wolves: Destiny of the Wolf, Wolf Fever, Dreaming of the Wolf, Silence of the Wolf; A Silver Wolf Christmas, Alpha Wolf Need Not Apply, All's Fair in Love and Wolf

Highland Wolves: Heart of the Highland Wolf, A Howl for a Highlander, A Highland Werewolf Wedding, Hero of a Highland Wolf, A Highland Wolf Christmas

Billionaire in Wolf's Clothing, A Billionaire Wolf for Christmas

An Excerpt from:
The Ancient Fae

The World of Fae
Book 4
Terry Spear

PUBLISHED BY:

Terry Spear

Discover more about Terry Spear at:
http://www.terryspear.com

ABOUT THE ANCIENT FAE:

Princess Ritasia misses the adventure of getting her brother and cousins out of trouble, but when the hawk fae king arrives to court her, she becomes involved in trouble nothing like she's ever faced before.

The hawk fae king, Tiernan, must find a bride, but being a tyrant king, or so his people believe, he must find a woman who would help him to change his people's view of how he and his queen shall rule.

Princess Ritasia isn't anything like what he'd envision his queen would be like. Rough and tumble, unafraid of danger, and speaking her mind, the lady might just be the one for him.

The princess believes the king is a tyrant, at least at times. But she discovers he's not all that he seems, and she wants to learn even more.

The problem is that Ritasia stumbles across an ancient queen's magical artifact and nothing will ever be the same between her people, his, and what is dug up at the ancient fae dig site.

CHAPTER 1

Overhearing her brother's raised voice in his bedchambers, Princess Ritasia could only guess who he was speaking to as she was making her way to her own bedchambers, intending to change clothes and take a jaunt somewhere, someplace forbidden. The corridor was cooler now with the advent of fall. The autumn wind whistled outside the ancient stone walls of the castle, filtering through every crack and crevice. The tapestries depicting fae on horseback hunting or fighting could not keep the cold from finding a way in.

She shivered in her pale blue gown and realized if she was going to stay in this part of the world, she needed to put something warmer on as the temperature had surely dropped even from the time she had risen this morning. Paused near her brother's door, she was not about to venture past it until she heard all that was said between her brother and cousin.

She *could* walk on past, so they could see she was here and could overhear them, allowing her brother to decide if he wanted her to witness the confrontation or not. But she wanted to know what was up as this affected her also. And she wasn't sure he would allow her to listen.

Since Deveron hadn't shut his door, how did he expect to have a private conversation anyway? The fault was not her own that she overheard them.

"Micala, you will not see Cassie any further. And *that* is my final word on it," Deveron said, his words harsh.

"She is waiting for me at the ice cream parlor in South Padre Island, as we speak, my lord. I have to at least go there and tell her something." Micala wasn't backing down, which wasn't really like him when faced with her brother's wrath and didn't bode well, though Micala couched his own hot temper with an attempt to make an appeal to the crown prince of the dark fae.

"I will not permit it. You were only to pay attention to the human girl a couple of times under my direct orders, not to make such a big deal of this," her brother snapped. "If my mother learns of your continued association with Cassie, your proverbial goose will be cooked. It does not matter that you're her favorite nephew. She will not permit it. Do I make myself perfectly clear on this issue?"

Micala didn't say anything in response. Ritasia barely breathed, hoping her cousin would agree with Deveron before it was too late. Deveron was right. Micala had no business seeing the human girl beyond what her brother had expected of him in the first place.

And with Micala's continued persistence in seeing Cassie, the rift between her girlfriend Alicia, who was Deveron's betrothed, and Deveron, was ever widening. Which really infuriated Deveron.

"I have to see her," Micala said, as if the prince had not just made a ruling.

Deveron's command was always final. Just as when their mother, Queen Irenis, dictated to her courtiers. The only one who could change his ruling was the queen herself. Micala knew that. Why was he being so obstinate about it?

Micala continued, "We were to meet at the ice cream parlor in South Padre Island. Let me see her and call things off between us."

"You should have done so long before this. I have warned you in the past. If you do not agree with my rule, I will call the guards," Deveron threatened, his voice low, dark, and perfectly even. She knew when he took that tone of voice, he was on the verge of throwing their cousin in the dungeon of the Denkar castle, manacled against fae travel until Micala did what was right. Though she knew Deveron only thought to protect him, to keep their cousin safe should their mother learn Micala was still seeing the human girl and growing too fond of her.

Ritasia liked Cassie, who was spirited and friendly, and she had no wish for her feelings to be hurt. But they were bound to be, one way or another.

"If you do not see her, she will be upset, Micala. But she will have to learn you are *not* coming back and move on. She will find someone else. Someone human. As it should be." Deveron was again the voice of reason.

Micala didn't respond.

"*Don't* make me force you to mind me," Deveron said, growling low.

"I will stay," Micala said, sounding highly frustrated. "If it pleases your lordship, may I leave?"

"By your own word, you will not meet up with her, Micala." Deveron waited for his cousin to agree.

After a long pause, Micala finally said, "Aye."

He sounded defeated, but Ritasia would try to smooth things out with Cassie and let her down as gently as she could while helping Micala out at the same time. She returned to her chambers to change clothes, so she could be dressed appropriately for the human world. Now that she had a real mission in mind.

She pulled out one of her drawers filled with human clothes and slipped out a shimmering blue bikini. South Padre Island was still warm this time of year. And then she grabbed a flowery silky sheer skirt sarong and a pair of golden sandals. Quickly, she changed out of her gown and dressed for the warm island temperatures.

She would see Cassie, tell her something—she wasn't sure what yet—and then Ritasia would have fun with a guy—beach-time cute. Only he had to be without a girlfriend. Many of her female kind wouldn't care if a guy was alone or not. They'd just butt in and stir up trouble between the happy human couple. If the guy was too fickle to stick it out with his girlfriend and threw her over for a fae, he deserved what he got.

At least that was most fae's feelings on the matter.

But Ritasia wasn't interested in getting a guy like that to take notice of her.

Though she was supposed to always have an escort with her, she had never allowed that rule to stop her before. Without a word to anyone, she transported herself to South Padre Island, planning to visit her favorite ice cream shop, locate Cassie, and commiserate with her about how unfaithful men were, then take off down the beach to look for a nice fun human guy to spend the afternoon with.

The warm salty air swirled about her, catching her silky scarf skirt and tugging at it, when she noticed the wall that had been illustrated with graffiti, compliments of the winged fae. It appeared that humans had finally managed to cover her cryptic fae message with several layers of white paint. At least she assumed they had. Maybe her own people had done it.

She turned to head for the ice cream parlor where she'd get a nice hot fudge sundae while she tried to make Cassie feel better. But as soon as she turned around, she nearly ran straight into an unseelie fae, who was invisible to humans. Why had the blasted unseelie not even attempted to avoid running into Ritasia? The unseelie had seen Ritasia first and could easily have moved out of her path! In fact, she should have gone far out of her way to avoid any confrontation.

Ritasia glowered at the fae. The unseelie's red hair was piled on top of her head with silver combs, her skin white, eyes ringed with silver, unlike those of the seelie whose eyes were ringed with gold when angered. Which meant the unseelie was in a highly irritated mood already. She was wearing a teeny weeny bikini of white that was barely big enough to cover all the parts that needed covering.

Although Ritasia was wearing a bikini also, as she planned to catch a guy's eye after she saw Cassie, and when she found the right target, her bathing suit wasn't half as skimpy as the one the unseelie was wearing.

The girl, not much older than Ritasia, gave her a harsh look in return as if daring her to do something about her behavior, then continued on her way. Ritasia glanced back to watch the unseelie, who were said to have once been part of the seelie court. But one faction split off from another and waged war for so long against the other, using magical weapons of mass destruction so that another queen could rule in ancient times, the fabric of the world had been ripped in two, creating two separate fae planes. And then of course there was the human plane where both unseelie and seelie could visit. But they normally avoided confrontation when they ran across each other in the human world.

Like the seelie, the unseelie could be good, and they could be evil. So, just being an unseelie didn't equate to all bad.

Ritasia watched as a young blonde, blue-eyed boy, studied the flight of a Monarch butterfly in his path, fascinated, chubby cheeks dimpled, mouth lifted as he walked beside his mother. And then the unseelie drew near him, and Ritasia knew she meant to do something bad. Kill the butterfly? Or something else?

Something else. She stuck her foot out and tripped him. He landed on his bare knees, bloodying them on the rough concrete sidewalk, and he started bawling.

Ritasia wished she could have thwarted the unseelie, although she knew it wasn't something she should have interfered with anyway.

The unseelie had moved past the boy, but looked over her shoulder to gloat at what she'd done, as if the deed had given her a bit of evil pleasure. Then she saw Ritasia casting her a devil of a glower. The unseelie offered her a simpering smile and blew her a kiss as if to say, *Love the humans if you wish, but they're in my way.*

Not that Ritasia didn't feel similarly when humans got in her way, but clearly the boy had *not* been in the fae's path. The unseelie could very well have stayed out of his way.

The boy's mother lifted him in her arms and cooed to him, and his cries quieted.

Not all unseelie were bad, Ritasia reminded herself. And it was none of her business as to what the unseelie was up to.

She turned around to walk to the ice cream parlor and saw a cute guy stalking up the sidewalk in her direction, tanned, tall, and dark chocolate eyes that caught her gaze, and he smiled. Now *he* was just what she had in mind. He could even buy her the hot fudge sundae, and then she'd see Cassie and tell her…well, she still wasn't sure what to tell her that wouldn't hurt her feelings too badly. But Micala couldn't see her any longer.

Suddenly the human guy waved in Ritasia's direction, and she looked back to see who he was waving at, figuring she'd already lost her prime catch for the day.

Then she saw who it was. Who else but that blasted unseelie in the too-small bikini! And now *she* was heading straight for him, a thin smile stretched across her face, her green eyes sparkling with the devil. She was now very much visible in that scrap of a bikini, waving at him as she hurried to join him.

He looked over his shoulder as if he wasn't sure she really meant him, but then she said in a sickly-sweet tone that didn't suit the witch, "Tom, is that you?"

He cleared his throat, his cheeks and neck tinged with color. "Uh, no, I'm Mike. I guess you thought I was someone else."

Ritasia wanted to laugh at the unseelie's attempt to woo him. He looked a little disappointed. Here he thought some really hot chick was interested in him.

The guy focused on the unseelie's barely-there bikini and more importantly, all her naked skin, when Ritasia made her move. Though she knew better. But the unseelie really irked her.

"Mike," Ritasia said, smiling brightly, walking toward him, too. Her bikini wasn't as risqué as the unseelie's, but Mike's tongue was hanging out just the same as his gaze shifted over her figure, then caught hold of her gaze and held it.

Yeah he was interested in her. Maybe her dark hair and eyes appealed more than the redhead's coloration. Or maybe he thought the redhead's bikini was a little too revealing, and he wanted a girl who wasn't such a show off. Or maybe he liked that she had called him by his real name.

He might have thought it was his lucky day. But when a seelie and an unseelie wanted to play with the same human, he was deadly mistaken.

Ritasia *knew* better than to make a move on him. She had been trained to avoid the unseelie as they seemed to have been taught to leave the seelie alone. But Ritasia couldn't help herself.

The unseelie *wasn't* about to let her prey go either though. "Mike, of course, from…" Ritasia hesitated, letting him tell her just where he was from.

"I'm a local," he said.

Wow, great tan, great body, *great* smile, Ritasia thought.

"I come here all the time," Ritasia said, which she did, when she could. "You could say I'm *almost* a local."

"Cool," he said, looking unsure as to who he should make the play for. It should have been obvious, Ritasia thought.

Then she smiled brightly. "When I was here last, you said you would take me for a hot fudge sundae."

The guy cast another 1,000-watt smile and said, "Sure," knowing he hadn't, but he seemed totally willing to play the fae's game. Humans always were. Hot guy, cute willing chick. Easy prey for a female fae.

The unseelie looked as though her wind-tossed hair could become writhing red coral snakes, and she would turn Ritasia into stone if she glanced in her direction again.

"Ritasia!" a male fae shouted.

Crap! Her brother, Deveron, his voice highly agitated, with an undercurrent of concern.

Ritasia swung around, her whole body heating. Deveron was dressed in jeans and a T-shirt and sneakers. He probably had gotten word about her being here unchaperoned and had thrown on some human clothes to intercept her. Unless…unless he was checking on Cassie and making sure that Micala hadn't popped over to see her despite Deveron's ruling. Maybe *he* was planning on telling her Micala couldn't see her any longer.

Deveron glanced at the unseelie, gave her a dark look, and spared the human an even hotter look as if to wordlessly tell him to leave before he really got himself into a pit of venomous snakes.

Then Deveron reached Ritasia. "We had a date, remember?" He sounded like a miffed boyfriend.

Her skin heating, she clamped her lips tight. Then she smiled, figuring a way to solve the issue of who

Deveron was and said, "Mike, I'll have to take a rain check. My brother needs me." She knew her brother would not permit her to stay. Not right now, anyway.

"Brother, my butt, *Ritasia*," the unseelie said, sneering.

"Princess to you, jealous fae," Ritasia retorted, before she could watch what she said.

The girl's brows arched. "Princess of some fantasy world in your mind?"

Ritasia glanced at the guy, realizing he was waiting for her to explain what she meant.

She couldn't.

"Come on, Mike. You can get me that sundae instead." The unseelie took his hand and pulled him toward the ice cream parlor, but he glanced back at Ritasia, and she knew he had wanted to be with her, not with the redheaded unseelie. Or maybe he was still puzzled about her saying how she was a princess and the other was a fae, and he wondered where she truly was from.

When they had disappeared inside, Deveron grabbed Ritasia's arm. "What is the meaning of you telling that human you are a princess and the unseelie was a jealous fae? I leave you alone for one minute, and the next thing I know you're trying to start a war with the unseelie?"

"One minute?" Ritasia shrieked. "You have not been around for days until you showed up this afternoon. And finally I see..." Well, she hadn't really seen him.

Only overheard him dictating to Micala. She jerked her arm free and folded her arms across her chest. "How did you know I was here?"

Deveron snorted. "One of our fae saw you and reported just the trouble you were about to get yourself into."

She wondered if Deveron had sent someone else then, to ensure Micala didn't try to meet with Cassie. Only instead he saw Ritasia mixing it up with an unseelie and returned to the castle to warn Deveron right away. "Which one was spying on me?"

Deveron smiled as if amused that she could not get away with anything. "I cannot say." Then he frowned. "Mother will have to find you work if you haven't anything better to do than start a battle with an unseelie."

"*Don't* tell Mother."

But the look on Deveron's face told Ritasia he might do just that. Her safety was always tantamount to him, which despite being annoying sometimes, she had to love him for his concern.

"Besides, another lord has arrived to court you," he said.

She groaned. "I will only say no."

He grabbed her arm again, and right before he transported them, he said, "I know. I don't like this one at all, so you have my blessing and my support."

"Wait!" But she couldn't tell him she'd eavesdropped on his conversation with Micala and planned to see Cassie to tell her…something.

Deveron didn't wait, but returned her to the castle, to the great hall instead of her chambers, where she scowled at her brother as the lord who had come to see her stared at her open-mouthed, eyeing her bikini and grinned.

Note to Reader:

The Ancient Fae is available now! I hope you have enjoyed the fae world so far. Many more to come!

Terry Spear